Charles Gibbon

**In Honour Bound**

Volume 3

Charles Gibbon

**In Honour Bound**
*Volume 3*

ISBN/EAN: 9783337196127

Printed in Europe, USA, Canada, Australia, Japan

Cover: Foto ©Andreas Hilbeck / pixelio.de

More available books at **www.hansebooks.com**

# IN HONOUR BOUND.

BY

## CHARLES GIBBON,

AUTHOR OF "ROBIN GRAY," "FOR LACK OF GOLD," "FOR THE
KING," ETC.

"A creature not too bright or good
For human nature's daily food ;
For transient sorrows, simple wiles,
Praise, blame, love, kisses, tears, and smiles."
WORDSWORTH.

IN THREE VOLUMES.
VOL. III.

LONDON:
RICHARD BENTLEY AND SON.
1874.

# CONTENTS OF VOL. III.

iv            *Contents.*

# IN HONOUR BOUND.

## CHAPTER I.

GONE AWAY.

LL the vague fears which had disturbed him during the night were
suddenly reflected upon his mind.
He heard the sob of the wind; he looked with
dazed eyes on the confused movements of the
fisher-folk ; he turned to the heaving sea, and
a thought which terrified him—which he tried
to beat out of his brain, took possession of
him.   Was he to take his place amongst these
mourners, not as their guide and comforter,
but as their fellow-sufferer ?   Had the cruel
sea robbed him also of his treasure ?

Impossible—she could not be so mad, so wicked as to venture upon the sea last night. Then he remembered her craving to know what lay beyond the horizon-line of her life, her passionate nature, and her indifference to the perils of the sea. If she could only have witnessed such a spectacle as he had seen that morning!

He did not know how her nature had changed since the birth of Baby; he still thought her capable of any wild act which might present itself to her fancy. He remembered, however, that there was no boat in the Witch's Bay now since the adventure of Teenie and Grace, and so he had one fear the less. She might have obtained a boat elsewhere, but that was not at all likely.

Then he was confronted by the enigma: What had she done? Whither had she gone? To Dalmahoy? To Craigburn?

No, she would not go to either of these places in the humour she was in last night;

and there was no other place to which there was the least probability of her going.

He thought, with bitter remorse, of the many trifling acts of neglect of which he had been guilty towards her; he magnified them into cruelties of the first importance. He thought of how often he might have given her pleasure when he had turned from her, complaining that she took no interest in his labours, and how important it was that all his thought and time should be concentrated upon the duties he had undertaken. He wished the old time back, that he might be more loving and less exacting. Ah, how kind he would be! how merciful to all her sins! how proud of all her pretty ways, and how blind to all her faults!

He thought of these things when it was too late; he condemned himself utterly and without pity.

" God help us, Ailie ; I fear we too have had a wreck last night."

" What's wrang—and what gar'd you ask

about Teenie, when you maun have been wi'
her a' night?"

"No—we quarrelled—I stayed in my room.
She did not go to bed. I thought she was
with you."

"God be here!" exclaimed Ailie, in terror;
"no wi' you, and no wi' me!—then she's
drowned!"

He felt sick as he listened to this echo of
his own first thought.  Both had remembered
her mermaid-like ways, and leapt to the conclusion that the worst had happened.  The
idea never occurred to them that she could
have adopted the common-place method of
travelling—on her feet.  As usual, in matters
of mystery, the wildest possible explanations
obtained the first attention, whilst the real explanation was quite simple.

His head bowed, brows knit, cheeks white,
and his hands clutching the staff which he held
across his body—as if holding himself in, trying by physical means to restrain himself from
any violent outburst of passion or grief—he

stood gazing at the sand; deaf now to all the din of wind and waves, of voices in sorrow or joy, and blind to the grandeur of the scene around him. The sun had at last overcome the mist, and burst in a broad golden glare upon sea and rocks, which sparkled and gleamed with many brilliant colours, as if the jocund morning were ready to make amends for the dismal shadows of the night.

Ailie was an active, bustling old wife, indeed she was apt to bustle too much, and to make everybody uncomfortable by her restless endeavours to keep everybody right. So she quickly recovered from her astonishment.

" It canna be, minister, that she's no in the house. She's just been making fun of you, as she used to do with me. Often she would go away for a whole day without saying a word, and for no other end than to have a laugh at me. She'll be hode somewhere about the house. I'll go see."

" Very well ; I'll follow you presently."

There was something unpleasantly quiet in

the way he said this; at the same time he raised his head, and the face was cold and stone-like.

As Ailie was hurrying off, he made a quick movement as if to stay her; but he let her go. His thought had been to bid her keep silent about the fears they entertained regarding Teenie; but then if she had really disappeared, the wider the fact was known the sooner she would be discovered. But his heart writhed under the sense of shame, and the prospect of the scandal which all this involved. There was a bitter feeling growing up within him, which made his blood cold, and gave an unnatural clearness to his thoughts.

He turned to the fisher-folk—they did not suspect how entirely he shared in their sorrows; they were grateful for his kindness, but they did not feel his sympathy so warm at this moment as they had felt it a little while ago.

"Go up to the station, Davie," he said to Tak'-it-easy, "and telegraph to Aberdeen,

Peterhead, Bervie, and to any of the stations they can communicate with, for early news of the missing boats. I hope we may have good news in a few hours."

Davie pledged himself to perform the task with dispatch, and to wait for the answers. He set off with what was for him a singularly swift step ; but on emergency he could exert himself like other folk.

Walter next gave directions about Red Sandy and the funeral ; ordered various comforts for the wife and bairns ; told those who were waiting in suspense to be patient—if they could ; that amendment came with bitterness out of his own suffering. But he was perfectly clear and considerate in all his instructions. He did not forget anything or anybody. The people who were not absorbed in their own afflictions or alarms, observed that he was " gey weary-like," but they supposed it was due to the exertions and anxieties of the morning. None suspected the anguish he was enduring on his own account.

When he had made all necessary arrangements for what had happened and for what might happen, he started homeward ; his hat was pulled low over his brow, his staff struck the ground heavily as if he needed support.

Passing through the village, he heard the shouts and laughter of children—a strange contrast to the lamentations on the beach below.

Habbie Gowk was marching down the street, strumming as loudly as he could " The Campbells are coming," on a Jew's harp, or " trump," as it is called; Beattie followed him, and on the back of the donkey were two touzy-headed girls of four or five years, whilst a boy of about nine held them securely in their places. A troup of children gambolled about this droll procession, shouting, and making fun of the poet and his companions. The twang of the trump was only heard at intervals above the din of the urchins. As soon as he saw Walter, Habbie took the instrument from his mouth and saluted him.

" Bad work down yonder, minister," he said, nodding towards the beach ; " I did not go after you, for I thought it would be ower muckle for my nerves, and I could do nothing. But it made me feel angry, the thought of it ; and what do you think I did ?"

" Went home to your breakfast, perhaps, and tried to forget that there was sorrow in the world."

" No, sir, I could not do that, seeing what I've been tholing mysel' for Guid kens how long. I just gaed up to that lawyer body, Currie, and roused him out of his bed—that would be good for him—I dinna believe he has seen this side of eight o'clock for years. He was for refusing to see me, but he was mistaken on that score. I banged intil his bedchamber, and got him in his night-gown.

" ' What do you want at this untimely hour of the night ?' says he.

" ' Night !' says I ; ' it's broad day, and I'm ashamed of a man come to your years to speak that way of the Lord's blessed light. I want to ken when I'm to get that fortune, and I'll have no more putting off's about it."

" ' How can I tell you ?' says he ; ' it depends upon the court : it may be next week, and it may not be for years. I've told you that often enough, and you're a fool, Habbie, to annoy me in this way.'

" ' A fool,' says I, looking at him as though it was at the far end of a fiddle, ' a fool in troth for listening to you. You've just worried the sowl out of me with your fortune ; but you can take it to the deevil if you like, for I'll have no more ado with it.'

" And with that I tramped out. It was a sore temptation to give him a walloping, for he had naething but his night-sark on ; but I thought of the bailies, and I resisted temptation. Outside, the bairns were cuddling Beattie, and wanting a ride ; so I put them on, and felt happier nor I've done since the day I first heard of the fortune. I would not take it now if they were to pay me for it. The thought of it has been naething but a misery to me, and now I'm beginning to feel like my old self. So we're going for a daunder."

Walter listened to all this as patiently as if he had no care of his own ; never attempting to interrupt, never displaying the least irritation. When he had done—

" I have no doubt you will be a happier man, Habbie, forgetting the fortune than you could be waiting for it. If it is yours, it will perhaps come to you in time ; but, at any rate, you can do without it; that is a great consolation. There are many to whom it would bring happiness : as it is, there are many to whom it has brought nothing but vexation."

" It's a' vanity, minister, and there's nae telling what a vexation of spirit it has been to me. But I'm for no more of it ; I'll sell my ballants, sing my sangs, and let the deevil flee awa' with the fortune."

" Where are you going now ?"

" Wherever the Lord wills and ballants may

be sold ; to the fairs and markets, and to see
our auld friends throughout the country. The
Lord be thanked we have no fortune to taigle
or fash us now."

" Will you go by Dalmahoy, and say that I
would like to see the Laird at once ?"

" I'll go to John o' Groat's if you like--
hereabout or far awa', it's a' ane to Dandy."

" Dalmahoy will be far enough to oblige
me at present.   And yet—yes ; I would like
you to go on to Craigburn, and tell Miss
Wishart——"

He stopped : Habbie filled up the pause.

" I was going there at any rate.   I want to
tell Miss Grace what I've done.   She's been
a good friend to me."

" She has been a good friend to every one.
I'll give you a note for her."

He took out his pocket-book, and wrote—

" In trouble.  Come to Drumliemont if you can.—W.B."

He tore the leaf out, folded, addressed it,
and handed it to Habbie.

"All right, sir; Beattie and me will be there in nae time. Am I to wait for an answer?"

"Don't trouble about that. Good - bye, Habbie, and success be with you wherever you go."

"Thank you, sir; it's rale kind of you to say the word—there are few folk ken what a lift a kind word is at whiles to a puir sowl. There's many a bonnie flower that would die for want of rain, but that the drap of dew comes and saves it."

"You are a philosopher, Habbie, as well as a poet."

"God kens what I am, for I dinna. Whiles I feel myself such a good-for-nothing creature, that I think it would be best to make a hole in the water, and have done; but then what would come of Beattie? that holds me back; and syne I hear a lad or a lass lilting one of my ballants, or see them louping wi' joy to the tune of my fiddle, or maybe to the twang of this bit trump, and I say to myself, 'Cheer up, ye deevil ; if you can make folk blithe for an hour or twa at a time, you're no such a worthless wratch as you thought yourself.' So I go on as before, taking my dram, and seeking sunshine on the hills and in the valleys, roosting in couthie farm-houses, or singing my ballants in a bothy. I never was downright miserable till I heard tell of that d—d fortune ; and I'm blithe again now that I have cast it overboard."

" You are fortunate in being able to cast your care overboard ; some people cannot."

" So muckle the waur for them. Good-bye, sir.—Now, bairns, you must get down, and you shall have another ride and another tune when I come back."

He helped the children to the ground with much gentleness ; gave one a pinch and the other a " kittle " under the arms, till they screamed with laughter ; then he mounted Beattie, and rode off to Dalmahoy.

Walter encountered Ailie at the gate. She had been looking for him.

"I'm in great tribulation, sir," she said; "she's no in the house anywhere, and the lass kens naething about her. · Oh, what have you been doing or saying, that the poor bairn should have been driven out of her ain house in such a night as it was ?"

He was not surprised by the information that Teenie could not be found; but he winced at what he knew would be the general exclamation—what had he been doing or saying to drive her away ? The blame and the indignation of the folk would fall upon him; nobody would take the trouble to investigate the real state of the case; and everybody would at once condemn him. Although he was ready enough to condemn himself, he disliked the idea of other people doing it, and regarding him as a monster. The disgrace of his position would soon tell upon him; right and left he would hear murmurs of reproach at his conduct; and he must be silent.

He could not defend himself without accusing Teenie, and that he could not and would not do. He must be silent, and wait with what patience he could command for the conclusion of the adventure. ·

She was gone: that was clear; and he must set himself to discover in what direction she had turned. She did not go by sea, because there was no boat; and if she had gone by land, it would be an easy thing to overtake her; but how was it possible to discover the route she had taken? There were no relations to whom she would go; and she had left not the least trace of her course.

It was a bewildering position; but once satisfied that she had not wilfully given her life to the sea—he argued himself into that belief with a dogged persistency, which indicated the trembling fears lurking behind it—he was disposed to regard her disappearance as a mere outburst of petulance, and he felt sure that she would return by-and-by.

Before Ailie he displayed no emotion, except what might be seen in the white face and quivering lips. But in his heart the struggle was terrible between his passion as a mere man and his sense of duty, reverence, and submission as a minister. He was trying hard to find the true path in this darkness which had fallen upon him. His wife had done wrong, and he was angry with her; but at the same time he felt that he, too, had failed. He was eager to discover in what, so that he might make all the atonement in his power. Still his heart felt cold and hard.

He had to write to a neighbouring clergyman, to ask him to officiate in his stead on the following day, for he thought himself quite unfitted to administer the Sacrament in his present mood. Opening his desk to take out paper, he saw the rough sketch he had made of Grace and Teenie in the garden at Craigburn, on the occasion of the first visit there with his betrothed. Then the old feeling of tender love came back to him and helped him.

Teenie's face seemed to be full of yearning and doubt; Grace's calm, and pathetically beautiful.   He remembered the happiness he had experienced when he saw that those two were friends; and his thoughts travelled on to the day on which they had come up to inspect Drumliemount.   He recalled the sweet promises they had exchanged, the bright hopes and dauntless faith which had inspired him.   And now!—those bubbles were very beautiful, and their existence very brief.

"Ah, my poor lass," he said, his eyes fixed dreamily on the sketch; "you cannot know how much I loved you, or you would not have left me.   You cannot guess how much my life was bound up in yours, or you would have forgiven me my sins against you, and tried to help me to accomplish some little part of my ambitious dream.   So you would have made me a better man, and made me love you more.   But the dreams were only dreams, and the reality is this!"

He glanced round the room, in which fur-

niture and books lying in confusion assumed
to his fancy an air of desolation. He put the
sketch away tenderly, and yet as if he could
not bear the sight of it. He felt that it would
do him good if his eyes would run with tears.
But they were quite dry.

# CHAPTER II.

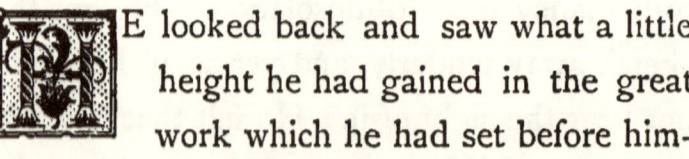E looked back and saw what a little height he had gained in the great work which he had set before himself to accomplish. He looked forward and saw the hills rise, height over height, until the goal was lost in the silver clouds of summer; so utterly beyond his reach, that it seemed as if there were nothing for him to do but look upward yearning, and die.

But this was the wicked prompting of despair—it was weak and contemptible. There was something better to do than yield to this weakness; he was bound to accept humbly and bravely the fate which was given to him, and to strive earnestly to do what was right and best under the circumstances, no matter what pain it cost him. He would try to do that.

He examined the bed-room ; she had not taken any extra clothes with her. He looked into a drawer where they kept small sums of money: she had not apparently taken any with her. Then she had not gone far, and she must travel on foot, or borrow a vehicle from some one who knew them. In that case they would soon trace her.

He tried to fancy in what position she had been standing in the room ; then how she had descended to the ground floor. He followed the steps, and suddenly he remembered that low sob at his door. His pulse quickened to pain in the bitterness of chagrin that he had not sprung up and saved her. What fiend of evil humour had kept him in his seat at that moment? The sob echoed in his brain; he saw her with hands stretched towards him, pleading for pity and forgiveness ; he had been silent, and she faded away into the mist.

"That is the true irony of fate—when it is busiest we are blindest," he muttered ; "God knows what mad act she may have been tempted to perpetrate, thinking my heart was changed towards her."

The cold sense of undefined fear again extinguished all angry thoughts regarding her.

At the door he encountered the Laird, who had been for the last five minutes listening to Ailie's description of the calamity which had befallen them.

The Laird was neat and spruce as usual, but the crows'-feet were more distinctly marked than they had been a few months ago, and any one seeing him now would have been able to make a near guess at his actual age.

"So," he said, his hands clasped behind him on the knob of his riding-whip, which he swung between his legs as he spoke. "So, the honey is all eaten, and there's only the bitter wax left in the hive. This is an admirable comment upon your grand contempt for my worldly and selfish counsels—as you called them."

" You counselled wisely, father, according to your view of things; I tried to act honestly, according to mine. I have not repented— Teenie was a good wife."

" Who the devil said she wasn't ? I think she was a splendid lass, and she would have made any man's home bright and pleasant, if he only gave her a fair chance. You cannot have done that."

" I tried."

" But trying is not enough—we must do. I am vexed about this squabble ; I like Teenie—why, her pretty ways almost per-suaded me that it was worth while losing an old family home in order to learn what real affection was; and she showed it to me, whom she had no reason to value much. What have you been doing to drive her away?"

" I cannot tell—I do not even know how the quarrel began ; but there were bitter words—the fault is mine."

The Laird looked at him curiously, observed the restraint he placed upon himself, and the anguish he was suffering. Then holding out his hand—

"Wattie, my lad, you're down: I won't strike. I'm glad you are so ready to take the blame to yourself. That's right: and now we'll find the runaway, and give her a sound rating for frightening us all."

Walter grasped the offered hand warmly. The two men had never thoroughly sympathized with each other until that moment. They were drawn closer together than ever before, and they seemed to understand each other better.

The circumstances of the disappearance were explained.

"It is a puzzle to know where to look for her," said Dalmahoy, "but you take the horse, and make a circuit northward; I'll take the gig, and go southward. We are sure to find somebody on the road who has seen her. What was the colour of her cloak?"

" Dark gray."

" That's not very distinguishing. Do you know what she had on her head ?"

" A Leghorn hat, I believe, with a blue ribbon."

" That's better. Now off you go—we'll soon find her. She must take the road somewhere, and there are only about a dozen roads for her to choose from. I'll get a gig at the inn, instead of going back to Dalmahoy ; and, I say, you'd better tell the women-folk here to hold their tongues, for the fewer who know of this business, the more comfortable it will be for Teenie when she comes back."

Walter saw the force of that suggestion ; indeed, one of the many disturbing thoughts roused by this escapade of Teenie, was that of the scandal which would spread throughout the county. " The minister's wife run awa'—ay, sirs, but it's a queer world." He dreaded hearing that exclamation, although at first, in his anxiety to find her, he had been disposed to brave it. But now, for her sake, he saw that it was best to keep the adventure as quiet as possible.

He arranged with Ailie to take the letter to the clergyman, whose friendly help he had asked for the following day; and he left a note for Grace, in the event of her calling during his absence.

Then he set out upon his sad journey. He took the old coach road first, and the fleet foot of the horse was very slow to his eager spirit. He reached over the neck of the animal, as if that would bring him the sooner to his object.

He drew up beside a stonebreaker, who was busy at work in a hollow by the roadside.

"Were you out early this morning, my man?"

The man dropped his long shafted hammer, and took off his goggles to have a good look at his questioner, whom he recognized, for it was only about ten miles from Rowanden.

" Ay, I was out at six."

" Many folks passed this way?"

" Oo, ay, plenty folk; there was Brunton's

cattleman; and there was a drove o' sheep, with the shepherd and twa dogs; and now there's yoursel'."

"You did not see any—women-folk?"

"Never a petticoat, and there's no ane like to pass without me seeing it. But there was twa strapping queans passed yesterday wi' their kists in a cart, flitting from Broomie-knowe."

"Thank you."

"Oo, you're walcome."

He passed on, up to Farmer Brunton's, where his inquiries met with the same result. Then he cut across country, pursued his search in a number of surrounding villages, visited strange farmhouses, and inquired at the cots of the labourers. Occasionally he found a woman at home in the cottages, who, after the first shyness and doubt as to the object of the inquirer, became loquacious enough about everything that had happened during the past fortnight—how the " clocking " hen had brought forth thirteen ducks,

and was "rale proud o' the clecking;" how
the sow's litter was likely to do weel; and
how the cow had calved in the middle of the
night, and nearly died.    But generally he
found in the cots only the bairns, whose
parents were out at work, whilst the household was left under the charge of a chubby
matron of eight or ten years.

The result was the same in every instance:
he obtained not the least hint about Teenie.

The day passed into gloaming, gloaming
into night, and still he was apparently as far
as ever from the object of his quest.

There was a curious stillness in the atmosphere, as if portending another storm.
The occasional chirp of birds, the call of a
man to his horses as he led them home, or a
brief snatch of a milkmaid's song, mellowed
and endowed with peculiar charm by place
and time, were the only sounds which broke
upon the quietude of the evening.    There
was a melancholy feeling inspired in him by
this awful stillness of nature.    As the shadows

darkened upon them, the mighty mountains impressed him with a sense of eerie solitude and grandeur. The white mist creeping slowly over all, enshrouding hills, trees, and houses filled him with sad thoughts. But it was the strange stillness which affected him most; it formed such a bitter contrast to the storm raging within his breast.

He had worn out the horse, and he was obliged to turn homeward, sick at heart, fagged out, and trembling at the rapid growth of his fears for Teenie's safety.

It was midnight when he reached Drumliemount. The Laird was waiting for him.

Each read in the other's face the answer to the question which remained unspoken on their lips—no success.

" I doubt we'll have to let it be known," said the Laird, with some impatience, in spite of his habitually philosophic (or selfish?) temperament. It was hard just at that moment to have an addition to the family troubles; and he could have delivered an excellent oration just then upon the value of submission to the experience of parents, but he refrained. "One advantage of making it known is that we shall be able to get information from all quarters, and also to make a thorough search of the district."

" It does not matter now who knows it."

" From what Ailie says, it is possible that she is hiding in some cottage in the neighbourhood, and laughing at us all this time " (the Laird did not believe that—he, too, began to have fears—but he thought there was no harm in saying it).

" Or she may be drowned," added Walter, in a low dreamy voice.

" Hoot, toot! no fear of that; we'll find her in the morning. You are tired; take a rest, and you will have more spirit for the work. By-the-way, have you arranged about the church to-morrow ?"

Walter took up a letter which was on the table. After reading it—

" No; Hutcheson cannot come until the

afternoon, and there is no time to seek any one else. I must officiate myself."

" That's awkward ; but the more need for you to rest. Come, Wattie " (pressing his arm with a half-shy tenderness), " let me guide you in this. Take rest, and whilst you are doing your work to-morrow, I shall be busy looking for her."

" You are very kind, father, and you punish me most in that way for the vexations I have caused you."

" Good-night," said the Laird hastily ; " do as I have advised you."

He went away, feeling anxious to help his son, and feeling very much pleased with himself. He did not remember the fib he had perpetrated to Teenie ; and even if he had, he could not have understood what an important part it had played in suggesting the mad course she had adopted.

Walter was utterly distracted by the combination of anxieties which surrounded him. The most solemn duties he had to perform in

the morning were so utterly at variance
with the disturbed and irritated state of his
mind.   He felt as if it would be an unpardonable crime for him to dispense the Sacrament, whilst his heart was torn by such
worldly distresses as those which now afflicted
him.

He had a very high ideal of the life he
ought to lead, of the work he ought to do,
and at present everything seemed to oppose
the aims which this ideal directed.   He was
conscious of two personalities—the common
one, which submitted to the buffets of the
world, and winced under them ; the ideal,
which indicated how he should endure and
rise above all the ills of life.   But everything
came back to the thought of Teenie.

She had done wrong.   Well, his duty was
to pity, to forgive, and to win her back by
love.   But she could not love him, or she
would not have acted as she had done.   She
had shown herself indifferent to his severe
trials—perhaps they were even the cause of

her flight; but he shrank from the meanness of that thought.

She had shown herself indifferent to the scandal which her conduct would create, and to the shame of it which must fall upon him. She had shown an almost unnatural carelessness about her child. Could he pardon this woman ?

The struggle was a fierce one, the hot passion of the man waging a great war with the high ideal of life and duty, by the light of which he had been striving to guide his steps. The passion was strong; the ideal light was pale. Passion led up its mighty battalions of wounded vanity; the sense of the ridicule to which he would be exposed; pride; rage at her trifling with the sacred ties of home, all combining in a grand charge of indignation at the doubt and slight of his love implied by her act.

No, he could not pardon her !

But the ideal and better self appeared, like a shadow in the mist, and reminded him of the sweet thoughts she had inspired, of the happiness of which she had been the source, of the tenderness she had shown him ; of the soft touch of her hand, the dear yearning light of her eyes; and his own eyes became dim, his heart swelled and throbbed.

The battle was over.   He rose up strong and brave, answering the problem he had to solve.

" Yes, thank God, I can pity—I can forgive her; I *will* believe that she has reasons for this conduct unknown to me.   I will trust her, no matter how bad she may seem to be . . .   My poor wifie, I will seek you and try to help you, not because it is my duty, but because I love you."

# CHAPTER III.

PALE blue cloudless sky, the sea bright green, restless as usual, but not noisy or fierce; a little cold, although flashing under brilliant sunlight; yet wearing a mild and winning look to those who were perspiring in the heat of the day.

A soft warm wind, which only at long intervals rustled the leaves of the trees; the warm drowsy hum of bees; the atmosphere quite clear, and presenting sharp outlines of distant objects. The roads like yellow ribbons fluttering in the wind, wavering downward and upward from far-away points, and concentrating at the foot of the hill on which stood the kirk. The hills, purple-brown and black in the distance, striped with streams which glistened and moved like quicksilver in the sunlight.

A slumberous sense of peace and rest pervading all, as if Nature shared man's reverence for the Sabbath.

The people, in twos, and threes, and fours, traversed the roads leading to the kirk with leisurely and contented steps, chatting quietly over the affairs of the household and the State, including the recent storm, and the damage it had done to the fishing gear and the crops. The farmers who lived at a distance drove in gigs at an easy trot; but some who were late came across the moor at a helter-skelter gallop.

At a quarter to eleven the kirk-bell began to ring, and the bells of Kingshaven joined heartily, if somewhat discordantly, in the chime. The Rowanden bell gave out a slow sharp twang, which would have been hideous but for the mellowing influence of the atmosphere. Bing bang, bing bang, bing bang!

That was the signal for the fisher-folk to ascend the hill. Being close at hand, they could afford to wait until the bell began to ring ; but at the first stroke they stepped out of their cottages in grave haste, and marched up the hill in a straggling line—those who had suffered and lost by the late storm, dark and sad ; those who had not been directly losers by " the visitation of Providence," blithe enough : it is so easy to bear a neighbour's sorrow. Those whose husbands, fathers, or brothers had returned safely and unexpectedly from the distant ports in which they had found shelter, were smiling with sweet content, although conscious that there were widows and orphans near them.

There was neither disrespect nor callousness in this—only the natural law which permits personal joy to predominate over sympathy for another's loss, and so prevents life from falling under an eternal shadow.

Most of the people entered the church at once, and took their places in the pews which

had belonged to the same families for gene-
rations.    But a few of the older folk lingered
in the churchyard, inspecting the graves of
departed loved ones, or gathered in groups
to exchange family and agricultural gossip,
until within a couple of minutes of the time
when the bell should cease tolling.

The latter saw the minister step out from
the gate of his cottage and cross the road,
his black gown gently ruffled by the breeze,
his hat pulled low over his brow, and his
head bowed, as if he were in deep thought.

The kindly recognitions given to him were
observed only at intervals, with a nervous
start, and a hasty "Good-day." For the
most part, he passed on, seeing nothing, and
entered the church.

The bell stopped, the doors were closed ;
there was a rustling of dresses, a preliminary
coughing, and the people settled down into
their places.

The dark-yellow-stained wood of the pews,
relieved here and there by a green or crimson

cushion, contrasted admirably with the sombre gray stone walls. Mottled beams of sunlight streaming in through the windows shot over the heads of the congregation, and imparted a degree of drowsy light and warmth to what would have been otherwise a cold and gloomy building.

A profound sense of the solemnity of the occasion was felt by the congregation; but that did not prevent several members from observing these facts : first, that the minister was pale and haggard-looking, and that his voice quavered strangely as he read the psalm ; second, that the minister's wife was not in her pew at the foot of the pulpit-staircase ; and that Dalmahoy's big pew in the loft was occupied only by his two daughters, Miss Burnett and Alice.

" Is the minister's wife no weel ?" was the question which men and women were asking themselves, as the leaves of their Bibles rustled in turning to the place indicated for the reading. A perfume of peppermint lozenges and

" apple-ringgy" (Southron wood) pervaded the mottled sunbeams. Outside there was a hum of bees. Occasionally a bee or a butterfly fastened upon one of the windows, and afforded much interest to the boys; in the distance there was a cock crowing with the most reprehensible forgetfulness that it was the Sabbath day.

It was in the prayer that the singularity of Walter's manner struck the people most. He began in a trembling voice that was scarcely audible. He seemed to wander, as if uncertain of what he intended to say; but gradually the voice became louder, the enunciation clear, and the tone so full of tender sympathy, that it thrilled the hearts of the listeners. Fervid passion combined with simple earnestness to give power and eloquence to his words. He cried for help to bear the ills of life with resignation; he cried for faith to strengthen those who faltered, to teach them that God was always near, however dark the night—however fierce the storm. He implored mercy for those whose affliction might render them temporarily rebellious, that they might be taught to see in their affliction their own errors, and to trust that whatever suffering He sends, He is ready to relieve. Faith, faith, faith! was his cry—the first condition of happiness, the first principle of true religion. He prayed that they might learn never to doubt His love, however bitter and apparently unmerited might be the misfortunes of this world.

There was a pathetic sincerity in the white face turned upward in the sunlight. It was the man's own sorrow he was uttering—his own faltering heart that he was helping. But each listener associated the words with his or her affliction in the late storm, and found comfort in them, and strength.

He made a deep and lasting impression upon his congregation ; he had never risen to the full height of the duties of his office until sorrow gave him power.

But throughout the day he found himself

again and again faltering, thinking about
Teenie; in spite of the exaltation created by
the sacred work he had in hand, the mere
man's nature continually asserted itself at the
most unexpected moments.   He was frightened by this weakness, and shuddered at the
thought of his own unworthiness to discharge
the solemn duties of the day.   He was glad
when it was over; still more relieved when
Mr. Hutcheson came up to undertake the
afternoon service.

He crossed the road hastily, and entered
the house without speaking to any one.
Weariedly he threw aside his gown, feeling
that he ought never to wear it again.   He
sat down, trying to think out quietly and
methodically what he was to do next, and in
which direction he was to seek her.   The
remembrance of the day filled him with pain;
he had gone through the most important service of the Church in a bad and unholy
spirit, his mind occupied all the time with
worldly anxieties.   He could only pray to be

pardoned whatever sin he had committed in striving to fulfil his task. He found it very difficult to walk straight.

Meanwhile there were friendly inquiries at the door, all loud in praise of the minister's eloquence (at the moment when he esteemed himself most incapable !), and anxious to learn what was the matter with Mrs. Burnett.

Poor Ailie, bewildered between her distress about Teenie and her desire to keep her disappearance quiet, betrayed everything ; but in such a confused manner that the inquirers went away, puzzled and in consternation, to spread the most exaggerated rumours of the calamity which had occurred in the minister's household.

The news soon went round : " the minister's wife had run away, nobody knew where to," and that was why he was looking so poorly in the church. Assuredly, had she been within a circle of five miles of Rowanden,

Teenie would have been speedily discovered. It was the one subject of conversation uppermost that day, and even prevailed over the events of the storm.

# CHAPTER IV.

RACE came at last. He knew who it was the moment she touched the door. He sprang up to meet her, but she was beside him before he could make a couple of steps; the delicate hand was resting on his arm, the sweet sad face turned up to his, the clear earnest eyes eloquent with sympathy and inspiring hope.

"Thank you, Grace," he said, taking her hand quietly; "it does me good to see you, just as much now as in the old days when you were my protector in every danger. You are very brave and generous—but brave people are always generous. I thought of you first as soon as I discovered what had

happened here.  I wished much to see you
yesterday."

"I was here twice, but you had not returned," she answered in her low, quiet
voice; "you did not learn anything about
her?"

"Nothing.  I am haunted by the fear that
she may have ventured upon the sea.  I say
to myself it is nonsense—that she had no
boat, and that even if there had been one,
she would not have used it on such a night.
But the fear comes back to me, and tortures
me."

"Why did she go away?"

"I cannot even guess her motive.  I said
very little to her; she was angry about something, and I left her, expecting that she would
sleep and forget.  I must have done something or said something that she could neither
forget nor forgive."

He walked across the room agitatedly,
feeling that movement of some kind was
necessary.

Grace stood looking at the window, eyes open, and apparently trying to catch some slippery idea that was eluding her efforts as the bright-winged butterfly eludes a boy, and is farthest from him just when he thinks it is safe under his cap.

"I must have done something," Walter went on, "to pain her terribly. It is always those we love who pain us most." (Ay, Grace knew that.) "And she did give me all her heart. I have been too gloomy for her bright nature—I have been dreaming too much, and have accomplished too little. I chose a profession in which it seemed possible to reconcile quiet thought with the full discharge of duty. Wrong in that—men must act rather than think, to do any practical good in the world. Wrong in that, wrong in everything; it is a little bitter, is it not, to have to acknowledge that one's whole life is a failure ?"

"Walter !"

That little cry of affectionate surprise pulled

him up more sharply than a volume of argument would have done.

"Forgive me; I never could speak of these things to any one but you, and it is an intense relief to be able to let out the gathering of painful thoughts into the ear of one of whose sympathy we feel sure. I have tried very hard, Grace, to do what seemed to be right, and the result appears to be failure in every direction."

"Time is on your side, and a brave heart will overcome everything."

"That is one of the platitudes with which I have been trying to console myself; but it has much more meaning when you repeat it, than when I say it to myself."

Grace caught the butterfly of her thought, and she took Walter's arm.

"We'll go out to the garden."

They went out, and arm-in-arm, pacing up and down the path between the gooseberry bushes and the strawberry beds, she spoke.

"I have a suspicion of what put Teenie

out of humour, and why she has gone
away."

" What ?"

" It was my fault."

" Yours ?"

" Yes ;" and at this point Grace stopped,
feeling awkward and unhappy, because she
had to speak of her mother.

" Well, how was it your fault ?" he asked,
after waiting for her to speak.

She faced the position with a calm, brave
voice.

" I told her that my mother had again refused to save Dalmahoy. Teenie has gone
away in the hope that her absence would
make mother change her mind."

That was a revelation to him ; he saw
and understood all—the scene with Dame
Wishart, Teenie's passionate, sensitive nature,
her anguish in the belief that she had been
the cause of the loss of Dalmahoy, and her
brave attempt to save it by sacrificing herself.
His grief was the more poignant, although he

did not know that other element which influenced her action—the belief, or half-belief (for it was only when angry that she really believed) that he had expected to obtain a large portion of the Methven fortune when he married her.

" Heaven sent you to be a comforter of the sorrowing, Grace," he said, warmly; " you have made me glad, for you have relieved me of a heavy burden of doubt. I thought she went away because she did not care for me; you have shown me how true her love is— God bless you, Grace."

She needed a blessing as much as she deserved it; it was because her own love was so pure and great, that she was able to divine Teenie's motive. The same motive would have instigated her to the same action under similar circumstances, although her calmer judgment would have shown her the foolishness of attempting to set matters right in that way.

Keenly as she felt the bitterness of her

own fate at times, she was rarely unjust to Teenie, and always liked her. As for Walter, even his apparent blindness to the acuteness of her suffering did not make her angry with him. She only wished that she could learn to like him less, and that the touch of his hand, the least tender look or word from him, would not thrill her with such painful joy.

" You will be happier than ever when this is over, and she will be more contented."

" I shall try to believe that; but the first thing is to find her. I am waiting for a message from my father; as soon as it arrives, I start again to seek her."

" You will let me know."

" I shall go round by Craigburn before coming home, if alone; if she is with me, I shall send to you."

They walked towards the house, and Grace went in, to see that Baby was properly cared for, just as the Dalmahoy ladies came sailing along the path in their newly-turned silks covered with white muslin. Miss Burnett

4— 2

carried her parasol before her as if she were making a charge at something, resolved to impale it; Alice fluttered hers about as if the force of habit were too much for her, and she was obliged to coquette even with the sunshine.

Having almost run the parasol into Walter's face, Miss Burnett halted and dropped the point of her weapon.

"How funny!—I did not think you were so near, Walter. It's very hot to-day. What is this dreadful news about Christina?—is it true that she has gone away without telling you?"

"It is true."

"It is quite a romance," murmured Alice.

"I call it a disgrace," said Miss Burnett severely, and the "giddy young thing" stood corrected, fluttering her parasol from one shoulder to the other, and fanning herself with a delicately perfumed lace handkerchief. "It would not matter if she was the only person concerned; but the whole family suffers by it, and it is extremely wicked of her. But what could we expect ? I would never run away from my home."

And the consciousness of virtue added several inches to her stature.

"I would if I got the chance, but not alone," tittered Alice, who was again reprimanded.

This was irritating enough to him, but he spoke quietly.

" Will you grant me a favour, Helen ?"

" Certainly, if it is reasonable."     .

" I only wish to ask you to say nothing about Teenie until she comes home."

" Oh, *we* have no desire to mention the subject ; but it is natural that we should be anxious about a matter which puts us all to shame. Of course, if you decline our sympathy, there is nothing more to be said. The man is waiting, so we shall go home at once."

Tossing her head, and sniffing the air as if to detect the contamination that must be in it, she went off to the carriage, which was at the gate. Alice, as she was about to follow, just touched his arm, and whispered—

" Poor Wattie—I *am* sorry for you, and for Teenie too. I loved her very much."

He walked with her to the gate, and was there in time to assist Miss Burnett to her place. She was not at all reconciled to him when the carriage drove away.

He was about to go into the house, when another interruption occurred.

Mr. Pettigrew, as behoved an elder of the Kirk, was amongst the first to catch the whispers of scandal concerning the minister's household ; and feeling a solemn duty incumbent upon him to admonish the minister or to sympathize with him, as might be advisable, and feeling it to be an equally important duty to be the first to discover the details of this romance (why should anything sad or bad be called a romance ?), took the first opportunity of speaking to Walter.

After much clearing of his throat and shuffling, he made his mission known. Was it true that Mrs. Burnett had—had, in fact, eloped ?

" Mr. Pettigrew," said Walter, looking him straight in the face with the grave pale eyes, which compelled the man to study the geological character of the gravel, "my wife has chosen to go from home for a time. She did not think it necessary to send the bellman round the town to advertise her intention. Do you think it was ?"

" Oh, not at all, sir—not at all, that being the case."

Walter did not choose to explain further, said " Good-day," and retired.

Mr. Pettigrew had an uncomfortable suspicion that the minister had been telling him a "lee ;" but he had not liked to say so Somehow he never could get on with this young man as he wished ; he never could tell him the truth—if the truths happened to be always unpleasant, that was not his fault—as he felt he ought to do, and as his position as a merchant and an elder entitled—indeed, called upon him to do. But he made up for his reticence here by speaking his mind with all necessary embellishments when he stood once more on his own doorstep, and felt himself master of the situation.

Walter saw in these incidents the indication of the petty annoyances to which he would be subjected for many days to come, and he felt keenly ashamed of being an object for scandalmongers to work their stupid will upon. His natural inclination was to turn his back upon the place for ever, and so escape the vexations which were in store for him.

Grace held up Baby, who crowed merrily, kicked vigorously, and tugged his father's hair. Walter kissed the child, and, looking at him, resolved that he would not shun the place or the people. He would remain there to confront the slanderers, to shield his wife from shame, and to enforce respect for her by the honesty of his life. They would believe her innocent when they knew that he did not doubt her truth.

Message from the Laird—

" Have discovered nothing yet; telegraphed to all the stations open."

Walter took horse, and started again in search of her.

# CHAPTER V.

HE fright which the "tattie-doolie" gave her, had roused all the superstition of Teenie's nature; there were, to her, voices in the wind, now loud and threatening, again low and wailing; there were fearful spectres in the shadows of bush and tree and rock. The voices commanded and implored her to go back; the spectres crossed her path, and the waving branches seemed like arms directing her backward.

She broke through all at first, and would go on; but voices and shadows persisted, and her heart echoed the cry, "Go back, go back," for Baby's voice seemed everywhere ringing in her ears. Then she hesitated, began to tremble, and sank down upon a stone, crying. The desolation of her position overwhelmed her, making the utterly vague nature of her quest plain for the first time, and she felt as if she were a little boat that had broken away from its moorings, and was being tossed about by the sea without any hand to help or to guide it.

Under the swift-flying black clouds, amidst those eerie shadows, listening to the loud wind, and to the deep boom of the sea— telling its grim story of wreck and death— she yearned for the child, the husband, and the sheltering home she had left behind.

She would go back, and yet she could not. She shrank and quivered with shame for what she had already done; she feared that he would mock at her, scorn her—she feared that more than all the terrors of the night, more than the apparent hopelessness of the journey she had undertaken. She felt now that it was stupid and ridiculous to expect to find her father any sooner by leaving home

than she would have done by waiting for him.
But then, if she could only hide herself, Dame
Wishart would relent, and that would accomplish all she wanted.   At the same time she
was frightened by that terrible feeling of desolation, and she started up to go home.

The petty feeling of shame restrained her
again, and she turned in the opposite direction.   The farther she went, the greater became her terror of returning, until she felt as
if she could do anything, endure anything,
rather than go home.   So she went on and
on, too much disturbed in mind to be conscious of physical fatigue ;  but by-and-by
Nature asserted itself, she tripped often, stag-
gered sometimes, and at length would have
fallen, but that she obtained the timely help
of what seemed to be a brick wall.

She had instinctively kept the coast-line;
the loud voice of the sea had, perhaps, unconsciously guided her.   A thick white mist
shrouded surrounding objects, so that she had
no idea where she was.

The dawn increased the whiteness of the mist, but scarcely helped to make objects more definite.

She groped round the wall until she came to what seemed to be a doorway. After a little hesitation she entered, groping her way along, but stumbling over loose stones. There was a dim light from above, and presently she guessed where she was—it was a deserted lime-kiln, which she had seen on several occasions when out driving with Walter. She crept into a recess, sat down leaning against the wall, and fell asleep in utter exhaustion.

A cold, damp morning, the sun fighting its way through the mist.

She started up, alarmed, stupefied, and shivering with cold ; stiff and pained in every joint. What terrible dreams she had been dreaming ! She had left home—she was hiding—the white walls streaked with a slimy green caught her eye, the cold wind penetrated her bones, and she remembered it all.

She had dreamed that she was dreaming—
that she was at home, near Walter, near Baby,
and the weary wandering on which she had
embarked had appeared to be only a painful vision.    Lo, that apparent vision was the
reality, and the glimpse of home and the
loved ones was the dream.

She could not go back now—it was too
late.    Walter would never forgive her—she
could not forgive herself.

She was cold and hungry; the miserable
cravings of appetite drove her to seek
some human habitation, when she most desired to avoid her fellow-men and women.
She passed out from the shelter of the
lime-kiln, and the cold morning air seemed
to bite through her.    She knew that the road
lay along the top of cliffs which overhung the
sea, now near, and again at some little distance from the water.    Occasionally she
caught glimpses of waves dashing high up
against the rocks, breaking in white spray,

and receding like a baffled enemy from the walls of a besieged town.

By-and-by she heard the blithe voices of children, who were engaged in a game of hide-and-seek, singing in loud chorus whenever the hider was discovered—

> " I see the gowk and the gowk sees me—
> A-tween the berry bush and the a-p-ple tree."

She hesitated a minute, but the voices of the children reassured her, and she advanced to the solitary cottage. Through an open window issued the sounds of vigorous scrubbing and of a girl's voice singing. The air was slow, and the words melancholy, as they were generally rendered; but the singer in this instance, to suit the activity of her movements, transformed the air into a lilt, and whenever she was scrubbing with special vigour she hummed or mumbled, instead of uttering words. The song in this new arrangement ran somewhat in the following manner :—

" Ye banks and braes o' bonnie Doon,
    How can you bloom—um-um, um-um ;
How can you chant, ye little birds,
    And I sae—um, um-um, um—um ?

" Um-um, um-um—I pu'd a rose,
    Fu' sweet upon its—um-um—tree ;
And my fause lover stole the rose,
    But left—um-um, um-um—wi' me."

Teenie's shy knock at the door was not heard at first, but when she mustered courage enough to repeat it, the singer ceased, and the voice said cheerily :—

" Come in, whoever you are ; what are you standing chap-chapping there for ?"

She timidly crossed the threshold, and saw a stalwart young woman, with flaring red hair, on her knees beside a pail, over which she was at the moment wringing a cloth, whilst she looked round to see who was the visitor. It was a bright, happy face, and its surroundings matched it admirably—a bed in a recess, covered by a patch-work quilt of many colours, in which there was not a crease ; a deal table, wooden chairs, and three-legged stools, all "clean as a new pin;" a variety of tins hanging above the mantelpiece, polished like mirrors ; a pleasant peat fire, over which hung on its cleek the porridge-pot ; the steel top of the fender rivalling the tins in polish ; the hearthstone newly whitened, the floor half washed, and everything presenting signs of cleanliness and content.

The woman's first look at Teenie was one of great surprise ; the visit of a lady at that time of the morning was very unusual, and Teenie's clothes at once indicated that she did not belong to the peasantry. The woman got up respectfully.

" Guid-morning, mem ; and what's your will ?"

Teenie was put out by this display of respect, and she felt it the more awkward to present her petition.

" I am on my way to Aberdeen," she faltered, " to try and learn something about my father, who is out whaling."

" Guid be here! do you mean that you're
to walk a' the way to Aberdeen ?"

" Yes, and I want something to eat."

" Ye'se ha'e that, but where do you come
from ?"

She hesitated, but answered truthfully—

" From Rowanden."

" You belong to the fisher-folk then. I
wouldna have thought it from your claes.
Thank goodness my man's a gardener, and
I'm no fashed about storms or bad fishings.
Come here and sit you down; you look
wearied, poor thing, and I dare say the storm
has taken some of your friends."

The woman became more familiar, and
most hospitable, as soon as she discovered
that the visitor was in distress about something ; and she made no intentional effort to
pry into her business, although she talked a
great deal. She gave Teenie a drink of
milk, which was very refreshing, and some
bannocks, with the advice—

" You're no to spoil your appetite, for my

man—Andra Fyfe, he's head gardener at Knockmaddie—my man will be in to break-fast in twa or three minutes, wi' a' the bairns, and you'll just sup a platel o' porridge wi' us."

When she had settled Teenie comfortably in a chair by the fire, she proceeded to finish the washing of the floor, talking all the time.

" And what might your name be, miss ?—you're no married, are you ?"

" Yes ; my name is Burnett."

" Married !—ay, ay, you're a young crea-ture to be a wife. And ha'e you any bairns, now ?"

" One."

" A laddie or a lassie ?"

" A laddie."

" Ay, ay, wha would ha'e thought it, and you that young-looking ! But I have six mysel'—two loons and four lassies. I was just eighteen when I was married."

" You seem to be very happy."

" Oo, ay, happy enough. I just try to

5—2

keep the bairns and the house tidy, and take things as they come. It's the Lord's will, you ken, whatever happens, and skirling never saved a sow from the flesher. Andra's unco particular ; but he's a guid sowl, though whiles he's ower guid at lifting his wee finger" (a euphemism for saying that he drank too much), "and then there's nae doing wi' him."

So Mrs. Fyfe ran on, her excessive energy finding vent in gossip or song, just as happened. She finished the floor, emptied her pail in the neighbouring " midden," wrung out her " clouts," and then arranged the table for breakfast : a row of yellow bowls, eight in number, with one more for the stranger. Then she took a basin full of meal, which she took up in handfuls, and allowed it to trickle into the water, which she stirred continuously with the wooden " spurtle," or porridge-stick. When the meal was sufficiently boiled, she lifted the pot from the fire, and deftly poured out the porridge into the bowls, proportioning the contents of each to the age of the children.

The husband arrived. He was a dour sort of man. He expressed no surprise at the presence of Teenie, but his furtive glances indicated his curiosity about her. Having learned that she was on her way to Aberdeen, and wanted a rest and something to eat, he said she was welcome. Then the bairns were called in, and ranged round the table. The man pronounced a long and earnestly-spoken grace, milk was served round, and all with good appetite supped the porridge.

Teenie was much benefited by the warmth of the house and the food, so that after breakfast she was quite ready to resume her journey. The peace and content of this home made her think bitterly that she had neglected something in the management of her household. But she could not redeem the past.

# CHAPTER VI.

OUR ANDRA FYFE, when he learned the destination of his guest, remembered that there was a cart going a few miles on her way, and, if she liked, he would arrange with the driver to give her a " hurl." She was grateful for this assistance, and also for the comfort and strength which she felt after the rest in the cottage, and her substantial though simple breakfast.

She shyly offered her half-crown in payment, but it was declined kindly.

" You'll need it all," said Mrs. Fyfe, flinging back her red hair, and restraining the obstreperous efforts of the youngest born to spring to the neck of the guest; "keep your siller, and God speed you on your errand."

Teenie lifted the child in her arms—a merry-eyed, white-headed little lass of three years—and kissed her.

"'Ou was geetin'—what for?" said the child, with sudden gravity.

The mother had observed that fact also, but had said nothing; and now she endeavoured to interrupt the child. Teenie answered, lowering her face as if to hide it—

" I am not well."

" Eh, and 'ou's had to take salts and sinny!" (a remedy for every disease with the cotters, and the little one's chief idea of torment). "Me geet when mither gi'es it to me, and whiles mither skelp Bessie and whiles gie's me a bawbee. Did 'ou get skelps?"

"'Something as bad," said Teenie, smiling faintly, and thinking how much harder to bear was a mental skelping than a physical one.

"And 'ou that big!—wish me was big as 'ou."

"And I wish that I was like you."

Bessie opened her eyes wide, and tried to turn back the eyelids, to express her amazement at that incomprehensible reply.

"Set her down," cried the mother, with a sort of proud deprecation; "she's just a torment wi' her clatter. I dinna ken who she takes the tongue from—it's no from my man, and it canna be from me!"

Andra might have told another story, but at present he was at the door, grumbling that they would be too late for the cart. So Teenie placed the child on the floor.

"It has done me good to speak to her," she said, with distant sobs in her voice; "she minds me of my bairn—at—at home."

She found a strange difficulty in uttering the word "home," for the dreary sense of desolation came upon her again; she felt that she had no home now.

"Poor lassie!" murmured Mrs. Fyfe, her

sympathy intensified by her suspicion that Teenie had not told her the precise truth about the object of her journey. " Is't the father you are going to seek ?"

" No—my own father."

" Poor lassie!" repeated the good-hearted woman, thinking that matters were even worse than she at first supposed.

But Andra, hearing this, turned back.

" Are you married ?" he asked gruffly.

The sad eyes looked at him with timid surprise at his sudden change cf manner, and he felt abashed.

" Yes," was the simple reply.

" Oh !" he exclaimed, and stepped back to the door, satisfied when he learned that the bairn had been " honestly come by," as he used to say of such matters. He was, in his way, a stern moralist, and—although his own first child had been born before wedlock—he would not have helped Teenie at all if her answer had been different.

" Will 'ou come back again ?" cried Bessie, clinging to her skirt.

" Maybe ; good-bye, Bessie, and I hope you will have a long, happy life. I'm obliged to you, Mistress Fyfe—thanks to you and your man, I feel a heap better."

" Lord be wi' you wherever you gang, and you'll ay be welcome here. I hope you'll meet your father. I'm doubting there's some sair trouble upon you ; but I'm no to fash you with ony questions. You'll come back, maybe, when you're all well again, and tell us about it."

This was spoken as they moved to the road, where Andra was impatiently waiting, and trying to preserve his temper by chewing straws.

Teenie said good-bye again to her friend in need, feeling all the time that she was not thanking her with anything like sufficient warmth, although she felt very, very grateful for the kindness she had experienced, and deeply affected by what she had seen and heard in the cottage. Mrs. Fyfe was quite content; she was not accustomed to much effusion, even of gratitude. Three of the bairns were standing beside her—the others had started for school, five miles off—and she uttered another hearty "God speed ye," as Teenie walked away with Andra.

He strode through a field as a short cut to the high road, where they were to meet the cart. Whatever might be the reason of it, Andra was not nearly so dour in manner now that he was away from his own house—indeed, amongst his cronies he could be merry enough. Although he did not attempt any conversation, he showed her certain trivial attentions—such as helping her over a ditch, or through a hedge—which she would never have expected from him. Men are so different when beyond the reach of the " guidwife's" controlling and subduing eye!

"We're just in time," said he as they stepped into the road; " yonder's Sandy Crab coming. He's a blithe loon, but there's nae ill in him, so you needna be skeared at anything he says."

Sandy Crab drove leisurely over the long straight road, sitting on the front of his cart, cracking his whip—not to quicken the horse, but to amuse himself—alternately singing and whistling, "When the kye comes hame." He was a fair-haired youth, with a round red face, in which there was much simplicity and good-nature. But Sandy was, according to his own account, "a de'il among the lasses," and he was proud of the many conquests he had made, proofs of which existed in the shape of locks of hair, photographs, crumpled bows of ribbon, and a garter! The latter he had picked off the barn floor on the night of a kirn (harvest-home), where the dancing had been fast and furious; and the fun he made seeking the owner won him several hearts, as he said. He certainly obtained several photographs before the next term, although every lass in the place disclaimed the ownership of the mysterious garter.

He wore a brown Balmoral bonnet, jauntily set on the side of his head ; a double-breasted jacket, the back and sleeves of which were of a thick woollen stuff, the breast of dark brown moleskin, ornamented with rows of big white pearl buttons, and a medal he had won at the athletic sports for throwing the hammer ; trousers of moleskin. He was a broad-shouldered, smart-looking fellow.

" Hey, Sandy !" shouted Andra, as the man approached ; " will you gi'e this lass a lift as far as you're going on the road to Aberdeen ?"

" That will I, my dawtie," was the answer as the cart stopped ; " loup in, my lass. 'Come under my plaidie, and sit down beside me, believe me—' "

He did not continue the quotation, for he caught sight of Teenie's pale and somewhat frightened face ; and he knew by her dress that she was not, as he had at first thought, simply a country lass flitting from one place of service to another. Many a blithe day he had enjoyed in the course of such flittings; but this was not to be one of them. Besides, she had no kist.

He jumped to the ground, took off the back of the cart, and made a sort of gangway of it, by which she could ascend, with assistance, and take her place on the bundle of hay which he arranged as a seat.

"Will you get in?" he said, sheepishly enough.

She hesitated a minute, and then advanced frankly. The two men, one on each side, helped her into the cart; she sat down on the hay. Sandy fastened on the back, and jumped up on the front board again.

"Good-day, mem, and a pleasant journey," said Andra, quite kindly; "I'll be glad to see you if you come our way again."

"You're awfully good, Mr. Fyfe; I wish I could thank you as I would like to do," she said in a low quavering voice; for the kindliness of those strangers, and her own utter inability to make any fitting acknowledgment of it, impressed her deeply. All the world had seemed so cruel to her a few hours ago.

"Say no a word about it," answered Andra.

He nodded, and turned away to his work as Sandy cracked his whip, and the horse started forward with long heavy steps, the cart jolting over stones and through ruts made by the rains.

She sat with cloak drawn tightly about her, head bowed, but occasionally glancing round in a vain effort to identify the part of the country through which she was travelling.

Sandy hummed or whistled to himself in an undertone, stealing many sheepish glances at the lady—for a lady she was, he had no doubt ; and he wondered much how she came to be a friend of Andra Fyfe's, and why she was travelling by road to Aberdeen, when there was the train to take her in a very short time. At length—

"Are you cozy ?"

"Quite, thank you."

The voice was a very sweet one, and the manner friendly; yet all Sandy's arts failed him, and he felt unable to continue the conversation. He had a series of jokes, which were always successful with the lasses; but this one seemed so sad that the jokes were damped. He went on cracking his whip— doing even that quietly—humming, whistling, and wondering.

She was thinking of the happy home she had seen that morning; how blissful was the lot of Mrs. Fyfe! how blithe the bairns! She could have been happy, too, in a humble cot like that, where there were no worries about money—no bitterness of disappointment about great fortunes, and where the round of duties consisted in keeping the house and bairns tidy, making the porridge and kail, and having a pleasant smile for the guidman when he came home from his work.

They were content—ay, there was the

secret of it all; and she had marred the happiness of her home, because she had not been content. Her heart swelled and throbbed as she realized how foolish, wicked, and wrong she had been in leaving Drumliemount. She wished she could go back; but shrank from that. The petty feeling of shame—of pride— barred the way. She *could not* go back now; it was too late.

But it was all so strange—the journey through the night, the rest in the deserted lime-kiln, the friends of the morning, the bright home, the bairns' voices, Mrs. Fyfe's queer song, and the jolting over the road in a cart. She seemed to be travelling in dreamland : it must be just one of those waking dreams which had so often visited her, and in which she had tried to see the strange lands and peoples of the ballads and fireside legends ; or tried to comprehend that vague yearning for the something beyond her daily life, which had been part of her nature since ever she could remember looking out in

wonder upon the moors and the restless
sea. There seemed to be always something
wanting to complete her state, to perfect her
happiness.

What was it she yearned for? Was not
this the expression of a discontented spirit,
restless and ever changing as the sea? Nobody had perfect happiness on earth, yet she
had been craving for it all her life, like a
child crying for the moon to play with. It
could not be love she sought, for she had
found that. She felt very miserable as she
began to think that selfish discontent was at
the bottom of it all. And yet she loved him;
she was going to prove that by hiding away,
by sinking utterly into the dreamland, so that
he might be happy.

Dreams, dreams, dreams! Presently Walter would speak, or Baby would cry, and she
would waken up in the dear home, and she
would be so practical and steady, that they
would all be glad this wandering had been
only a dream.

"What way do you no take the train to Aberdeen?"

That was a voice far away; but it reached her, and was slowly drawing her down from the clouds to the everyday commonplaces of her position.

" Are you sleeping?"

The voice was louder and much nearer.

" ' Oh, are you sleeping, Maggie?' " sang the voice, and went on with the rest of the verse.

She raised her head drowsily, and saw the ruddy face of Sandy Crab, bent towards her, laughing.

" I'm wae to rouse you, for you look weary," said the rustic beau; "but unless you mean to gang up to the hill with me, and help to load the peats, there's nae help for't. We're near as far on your road as I'm going. You'll never tramp to Aberdeen; what way do you no take the train?"

The repetition of the question roused her to its significance. The train?—she had

never thought of it ; all her ideas had been so
confused; she had only wished to get away
from Drumliemount, and to move towards the
granite city in the faint—almost absurd—hope
that she might there learn something of the
" Christina." Her distress had been too
bitter, her mind too much distracted to form
any definite plans as to her movements.

" I don't know," she answered, shame-
facedly ; " I—I did not think of it."

" Od, that's queer; but it's your best
plan."

" Where could I get the train ?"

" At Steenhyve, about six miles from here ;
but if you take the footpath through the
wood, it's not more than four and a bittock."

" What is the fare ?"

" I'm no sure, but about half-a-crown, I
dare say."

That was just the sum of which she was
possessed : she would have nothing to give to
Sandy, and she would arrive in a strange city

penniless. But it was best to hasten her journey, and she would not think of what was to happen when she reached the end of it. She was still dreaming.

The cart stopped at the corner of a narrow road, which led up to the hills whither Sandy was going for peats. He dismounted, took off the back of the cart, and offered his assistance to her in descending to the ground. She just touched his shoulder, and jumped down.

" You loup like a two-year-old," he said admiringly; " by my sang, I would like to hurl you all the way to Steenhyve; but I've a long road to go yet, and I maun be hame before even. The work has to be done, you see, whether we like or no, and I'm no one of those lazy beggars that just says, Come even, come saxpence" (meaning that the day's wage is paid whether the work is done or not).

" You have given me a good lift, and I've had a fine rest, thank you," she said, " and I would not like to take you off your road.    I'll easily walk to the train."

"Go down there, then, till you come to a slap" (opening) "in the hedge, syne follow the footpath through the wood, and across the bog, and you'll come on to the road.    Syne turn to your left, and you'll come into the town.    You canna go wrong in broad day-light, although many a one has lost theirsel's there at night."

"I'll remember what you say ; but—how am I to pay you ?"

"Hoots! I need nae pay; I was coming this gate anyway ; but if you'll gi'e me some-thing to mind me of you—a bit ribbon, or anything—I'll be rale proud."

She gave him a bow which was fastened on the breast of her dress : it seemed to her very little, and she was somewhat astonished by the request.    But she took it as a simple desire for a remembrance of one to whom he had done a kindness, and she did not hesitate.

Good-bye was said—merrily on his side, as

he pinned the bow beside his medal; earnestly on hers—and he drove off to the hills, quite proud of his new trophy of conquest, as he regarded it. He was an irresistible chap among the lasses according to his own belief; but, then, very little satisfied him!

She walked down the muddy road, which was pock-marked by the steps of a drove of sheep not long gone by. The opening in the hedge was easily found, and she took the footpath into the fir-wood.

The trees were jewelled with rain-drops sparkling in the glimpses of sunlight which broke through the heavy clouds at intervals; again a gust of wind shook the branches, the heavy drops fell in showers, and there was a patter in the underwood as of children's feet.

Light and shadow played about the trunks, and there was a fresh, grateful odour in the wood. At first she walked upon soft moss or long thick grass, because the footpath was so miry; but presently the ground beneath the trees became bare and brown, relieved only now and then by a little patch of moss, or a group of fungi, and in one part by a solitary wild flower, which lifted up its head courageously to brighten this dark place, and caught new beauty in its solitude as a ray of sunlight fell at its feet to comfort it. Teenie stooped as if she would kiss the flower, but she did not pluck it; she left it there to cheer the path of whoever followed her.

Walter was riding along the road, passed the gap in the hedge, and yet he divined nothing of her neighbourhood. No instinct told him that she was near; his horse's hoofs tramped out her foot-prints, and he did not know.

Half an hour earlier, and he would have found her parting with Sandy Crab; but the latter was now a mile or more on his way to the hills, and she was in the centre of the wood.

# CHAPTER VII.

HE footpath became more difficult to discern as she advanced, and at last all traces of it disappeared. She turned back to seek it—failed ; thought she had gone a little too much to the right, and so turned to the left—with no better success. She was puzzled—looked all round ; but each direction seemed to be so like the other, that it was impossible to decide which way to turn. Long rows of bare trunks, light and shadow, the brown mould underneath— nothing sufficiently distinctive to guide a stranger to the place.

After a little hesitation, she marched straight forward. An hour's walking, and

.she emerged from the wood upon a narrow road scored with deep wheel-ruts, and having a ditch on either side.

She was tired, and rested there, sitting on a stone, leaning her back against the bole of a tree, and a black shadow shooting aslant her face and body. Hands resting limply in her lap, head thrown back, and eyes half closed. A sunbeam fringed the shadow, but did not dispel it. There was a warm drowsy moisture in the air, and she sank into dream-land again—the region of constant endeavour without accomplishment. She felt, as one frequently does in dreams, like one trying to escape some danger that was all the more terrible because of its vagueness; but her feet were heavy, and, try as she might, there seemed to be no possibility of moving beyond reach of the enemy. She was sensible of deep depression; she wished to get away, and could not.

She hoped that some one would pass, and direct her to the right road for Steenhyve;

but no one came. The birds were making merry overhead, and she sat so still that one little fellow dropped down beside a pool almost at her feet, and bathed himself with much fluttering of his plumage.

At length she got up, and resumed her journey, taking what she thought was the right way, but utterly indifferent as to her course, she felt so weary in body and soul.

The direction she had taken was towards the hills; but it was late in the afternoon before she became aware of that, and then she was utterly worn out, ready to lie down by the wayside and die. If it were not that Walter must hate her now, that he would spurn her from him, she would crawl back to the home which became dearer and more beautiful to her the farther she strayed away from it, and crave his pity—even that she would be satisfied with now.

But it was for his sake she had left—for his sake she must keep away. She felt stronger in thinking of that. Presently she was bewildered and weakened again by the disagreeable question, what was she to do, without money or friends, until her father returned ?

Still, it was for his sake : she would think of that and nothing else ; and so she would be able to carry out her resolution.

She came to a clear spring, sparkling like silver, in a hollow by the roadside; and standing over it, leisurely filling a brown pitcher which had a broken mouth, were two children —ragged, dirty, bareheaded—with black hair, almost white with dust, and unkempt for many a day. They were swarthy-looking, thanks to the sun, and quite as much to the dirt which seemed to be engrained in their skin. One was a boy between ten and twelve years, the other a girl about nine.

Their features were sharp and old-fashioned ; their eyes bright and dark. They looked healthy, in spite of the dirt. One moment they were laughing and admiring themselves in the mirror of the spring—

the girl was trying to arrange her brush-like hair in ringlets—and the next they were quarrelling about who should carry the pitcher.

" I carried it last time," cried the boy.

" No, you didna, and you're just a big lazy sumph."

" Say that again, and I'll gi'e you a clyte on the side o' the head."

Instead of saying it again, she put out her tongue at him ; and he might have fulfilled his threat, but they were interrupted by Teenie asking for a drink. The children displayed no surprise at her sudden appearance, but they gazed at her boldly. Then the boy—

" Do you mean out o' the pig ?" (pitcher). " You'll have that, but it's a far better drink if you put your head down and lick it up out o' the well."

" Do you no see the leddy would weet her bonnie ribbons ?" said the girl.

The boy was reasonable, and at once saw the force of that argument. He lifted up the pitcher. Teenie knelt on a stone, and avoiding the broken part, placed the edge of the vessel to her parched lips, the children examining her curiously all the time. He held the pitcher so poised that she could take what she required without inconvenience.

"Had enough?" he asked, as she drew back her head; and added, encouragingly, "There's plenty more."

She thanked him, and felt much relieved. She inquired the way to Steenhyve.

"I'm no sure, but it's a bittock from this. My father could tell you, for he kens every road in the country; but this is Saturday, and he aye gets fou' on Saturday. Mither will do, though; come on and see."

He took the pitcher and marched on ahead, Teenie following and talking to him; the girl coming last, in order to inspect the stranger's dress.

"What is your name?"

"Willie, and my father is Will Broadfoot."

"Where do you live?"

" Everywhere, frae Yetholm to Johnnie Groat's. We ha'e a house that gangs on wheels."

He said that with much pride.

" On wheels ?"

" Ay, yonder it is."

He pointed to a dingy-looking caravan which stood at the corner of a field ; a bare-boned, half-starved horse grazing near it on the roadside.

A woman sat on the wooden steps which led up to a miniature door. She was nursing a child, or rather, she was allowing it to lie across her knees, whilst she employed her hands in washing and scraping potatoes, which were in a tin basin at her feet. A dark, haggard face; her hair, untidy as the children's, had once been black, but was now streaked with gray, and was further altered in colour by the dust which had been allowed to fasten upon it. Round her neck was a string of bright red coral beads ; a red shawl crossed her shoulders and breast, passed under the arms, and was tied in a big knot behind; her skirt was of a thick brown stuff, much faded.

Teenie did not like the appearance of the woman, or of the house on wheels. She should have seen the latter at night in the village market stand, when the back was let down to form a stage, lit by four flaring and smoking naphtha lamps, which showed piles of Sheffield cutlery, warranted; Brummagem jewellery, watch-chains, dog-chains, work-boxes, mirrors, brushes, tea-trays, and the endless variety of nicknacks with which the country folk were tempted by Will Broadfoot, the most notable of gipsy cheap Jacks. Then the caravan looked brilliant, and the gaping crowd were too much interested in the jokes and drolleries of Will to notice the haggard woman sitting grim and silent in the background, handing out the various articles as they were required. Light and laughter in front, and she a sad shadow behind.

Without lifting her head, or pausing in her

occupation, the woman glowered at Teenie as she advanced with the children.

" Father's no here," said the boy, as if he were well pleased with the absence of his parent; then stepping up to his mother, " There's the water, and here's a woman wants to ken the road to Steenhyve."

" Ten miles or more," answered a low, harsh voice.

Teenie's limbs bent under her at that announcement. Ten miles! and she was already aching in every joint, with pains more acute than she had ever felt before. She felt sick, and was speechless.

" Take the bairn, and I'll let her see the road."

Teenie saw a wee pinched face, lifted up with a feeble smile to Willie. The face was that of a boy of four years, the body was so shrivelled that it was no bigger than that of an ordinary child of ten months. Willie raised his burden easily; the child was so light that a baby might have carried him.

"He's got spinal complaint, and there's a kind o' fever on him the-now," explained Mrs. Broadfoot—Agg she was called by those who knew her, Nagg she was playfully called by her husband. She rose to her feet, a potato in one hand and a knife in the other. She spoke with what seemed such callousness to the boy's ailment, that the listener shuddered.

Agg went on—

"You go down the road, and take to your left by the beltan of wood; follow the road, keeping the wood on your right, till you come to the auld coach road. Turn to your left again, gang straight forrit, and you'll come into the town. Look, yonder are the kirk-steeples."

Through the haze in the far distance, over wood, meadow, and moor, Teenie dimly descried the steeples of the town. Trying hard to remember the directions given to her, she said, weariedly—

"Let me rest here awhile."

"Rest," was the answer. Agg sat down on the step again, and proceeded to prepare the potatoes as if she were unconscious of the presence of any one; never looking up, although she was taking furtive glances at the stranger, and would have been ready to identify her anywhere—never uttering a sound.

Teenie sank down on the grass. She took off her hat—a broad-brimmed Leghorn, trimmed with roses and a blue ribbon—and tried to realize her position. But she was very weak, and instead of thinking about her own affairs, she was watching Willie nursing his sick brother.

Willie was chattering to his nursling, and—rude as he had been to his sister at the well—was treating him with loving care. He was plucking reeds and wild flowers to amuse him, and trying to coax a smile from him by tickling his nose with blades of grass. Two shrivelled little arms crept out from the dirty shawl which enveloped the child, and wee worn fingers touched his grimy cheeks affectionately.

" Bonnie Boolie!" said the faint voice tenderly—through all the dirt and rags the helpless one saw beauty in those who loved him—" you're awfu' guid to Patsy, and Patsy's gaun to dee. Whar do you think they'll bury him ?"

" In the moon, and there'll be bonnie starns for his gravestane. But we canna do that enow, so you're going to live to be a big man, and help Boolie to fecht the bubbly Jock [turkey cock] at Jedburgh."

" That would be fine fun," said Patsy, smiling wanly at the idea of him being able to help his big brother and nurse in any-thing.

" Will it no ? and father will dance a fling on the tap o' the house, and take a smoke frae the lum."

The withered frame shook with laughter at this conceit, and the child murmured again—

" Bonnie Boolie !"

" Come awa' down to the burn, and you'll catch a lot o' minnows," said Willie blithely, as if he were speaking to a companion as active as himself.

He carried the child down to the burn, always maintaining the fiction that Patsy was going along without being carried ; and then he caught minnows, and pretended that it was all Patsy's doing. The child quite understood the farce, and loved Boolie all the more, clinging to him as he had never clung to mother or father.

Teenie was very weak, and she wept, listening to the children's talk. The tears did her good. Mrs. Broadfoot went on with her work apparently unmoved, but her eyes brightened when she was shyly asked if she could change half-a-crown. She placed two shillings and a sixpence in Teenie's hand without a word ; but she tried the coin with her teeth suspiciously.

Teenie went down to the burn where the

children were playing, and gave Willie a shilling. He was amazed at this wealth—he had never before possessed so much all at once.

"I can do what I like with it?"

"Yes."

"What would you like, Patsy—tarts or sweeties?"

She took the helpless child in her arms, and fondled him tenderly; somehow, love had cleansed the poor thing of dirt, and made his rags appear as good as purple and fine linen.

"I'll keep the shilling," said Willie gravely, "as a luckpenny, and to mind me o' you—it maun be a lucky penny when you're that guid."

She kissed them both, and said good-bye. Willie hoped she "wouldna catch the fever," and wished that she could bide near them.

She walked briskly enough for a quarter of a mile, but her limbs were feeble, her feet faltered, and she knew that it was impossible to tramp as far as the town that night. Happily she reached a little inn, and there obtained a bed.

In the morning her joints ached still more than yesterday, and there was a severe pain at her heart.

The kindly mistress of the inn insisted that she was too weak to resume her journey, to say nothing of the wickedness of doing so on the Sabbath day.

A day and a night of physical torture that would have been unbearable but for the unutterable agony of her mind.

Monday morning she started. She tried to eat the breakfast provided for her, but could not. She offered the landlady a ring, one of Walter's gifts, in payment of her debt; but the good woman refused it, saying that she would trust her, and only asked for her name and address. After some hesitation she complied—it never occurred to her to give a false name—and then she went away. But the pains of body and mind were very

acute.   She could not understand herself, the
sensations were so strange.   She seemed
unable to walk.   At the corner of the road,
beside the wood, she saw a man who was
kneeling upon the ground, and bending over
a prostrate donkey.

# CHAPTER VIII.

## FAILURE.

"BEATTIE, man, Beattie; what are you so thrawn for? Can you'no speak to me? Do you no mind that it's market-day at Abbotskirk, and if you dinna look sharp, we'll no get there afore nightfall? Fient a ballant will we sell then; and where's our supper to come from?"

He spoke as if he were reasoning with a refractory child; but Beattie never stirred a muscle.

"What's wrang with you, man? You never played me a trick like this afore. Poor sowl, I ken you've had hard work and scrimp fare; but there's a guid time coming now we've got rid of that confounded fortune; so rouse up, and let's be travelling."

Hàbbie took off his cap, and drew his sleeve across his brow to wipe off the perspiration. He looked puzzled and distressed; he glanced round him as if seeking relief from the green fields and trees.

He saw Teenie, who was standing near, uncertain whether to make her presence known or to run away. But her heart yearned for the sound of any familiar voice, and so she remained, wondering at Habbie's strange address to the donkey.

"Guid be here, Mistress Burnett, where did you drop from?"

She hesitated; then, awkwardly—

"I am on my way to Aberdeen, to see if there is any news of my father."

"Eh!—you're a long way off your road, then."

"I—was walking and—missed the road."

"Walking!—and where's the minister?"

"At home—I suppose."

Habbie was quick enough to see that there was something out of joint; but he only scratched his head, and regarded her with a perplexed expression.

She took a seat on a green knoll near him, and began in a weary, abstracted way, to pluck handfuls of grass.

"Yon was awful work the storm made," he said, watching her curiously.

"What did it do? was anybody lost?"

"When did you leave hame, that you dinna ken?"

She felt herself caught, but she was indifferent now to everything.

"On Friday night," she answered, carelessly.

"In the name of the Lord, what's wrang with you, mistress? I ken by your looks, and by what you say, that there's trouble of some kind. What is it?"

"Nothing—only I want to—I want to go on," was the lame answer. Then, as if afraid of herself in asking such a question, and turning her head aside, " When—did you see Mr. Burnett ?"

" Saturday morning, working hard to comfort them that were sorrowing through the storm."

His words recalled vividly the pale anxious face and the loving eyes of Walter, striving earnestly to discharge the duties of his office, however much his own heart might be racked. She had been thinking of him and of Baby constantly ; but the presence of one associated even remotely with the old home-life made the memory keener, and the sense of all she had sacrificed the more bitter. If it had been to do again, she did not think she would have strength for it. How the memories of his kindness crowded upon her—the bright vision of home—its tender anxieties, sweet though troublesome—the cry of Baby—the quiet evenings, which had sometimes seemed to her wicked nature dull—all filled her heart with yearning regrets. Elbows resting on her knees, hands covering her face, her bosom heaved with suppressed sobs.

"Beattie and me gave up the fortune at last," said Habbie, as if seeking to relieve her by changing the subject of conversation; "and we came away for a daunder through the country. We've been blithe billies, I can tell you, till this morning, when Beattie looked queer, as though he wasna weel. We came on right enough until he lay down here; and he'll no speak to me.—Do you no hear me Beattie?—Lord be guid till us, he canna be dead!"

He had been patting and coaxing his old friend as he might have done to a child in a pet; but Beattie lay so quiet and pulseless that at length the truth flashed upon him, and he drew back like one stunned by a blow.

His cry was so piteous that Teenie lifted her head and looked at him. He was sitting in a sort of stupor, glaring at Beattie, trying to cheat himself with the fancy that he still

saw signs of life. Teenie's love of animals
enabled her to sympathize with Habbie's distress. She went over to Beattie, touched him,
and knew that the faithful donkey had for-
saken his friend.

" Beattie's dead !" muttered the poet, wist-
fully, and for a little while he repeated the
words to himself, as if trying to comprehend
them. " Beattie's dead !—Ay, man, and
you've gane awa' that way, without ever a
word of warning. But I winna blame you :
you've been a guid friend and a faithful to
me, and the roads and the nights will be
driech and dowie without you. It's that fortune did it; I've seen it wearing you to skin
and bone, and breaking your heart as it was
doing mine. Poor Beattie; many a weary
gate we've wandered thegither, and some
blithe days we've had, too; and you were
aye guid to me, auld friend ; and I wasna ill
to you, was I, now ? But that's a' bye. I'll
never be able to make a song again, and I
might just as weel be lying down aside you."

It was the last feather which broke the poet's back. He could whistle at the disappointment regarding the Methven fortune, and thank Heaven that he was released from all anxiety about it ; but the loss of his old comrade and helpmate was hard to bear. He patted Beattie's side tenderly, muttering to himself in a dreamy way, " Ay, and Beattie's dead !—poor sowl."

By-and-by he turned to Teenie, with a feeble effort to grin at the absurdity of his own conduct.

" You'll think I'm crack, Mistress Burnett ; and maybe I am ; a' folk are crack, more or less, on one subject or another. Beattie was father, mother, brother, and sister to me. Twenty year we've been comrades ; there's no a road in the twa counties that we have not travelled thegither—no a house that did not ken us ; nobody will ken me now. He was getting auld, no doubt, and I did not make allowance for that ; but he's a guid creature, and he'll no set that down against me. He was just a poem on four legs, he was that kind and patient. Many a time he's gar'd me wish that men were donkeys, for syne we'd have honest folk to deal with."

He got up, looking at Beattie still, as if he could not believe that they were separated for ever.

" We must give him decent burial, any way. Will you wait there till I come back ?"

Teenie assented, and he hirpled sadly along the road to some cotter-houses about a quarter of a mile distant. The brown and green spotted thatch of the cots was shadowed by the trees ; a tiny burn ran past the doors, the clear water glistening, and making a merry tinkling sound, which the children fancied was the patter of fairy feet. He borrowed a spade and returned. Then he dragged Beattie a little way into the wood, and stopped at the foot of a tall fir-tree, on the bole of which the sun was glancing brightly.

" This will do ; the sun will come to him

whiles; and he was that fond of sunshine! You should have seen him when he was resting, the way he would roll on his back and kick up his heels, and laugh just in sheer joy and gratitude for God's bonnie light. But it's a' bye now."

He began to dig. The earth was soft, owing to the recent heavy rains, and the work went on rapidly. Pausing in his task, and resting on the spade, he looked up at Teenie.

"Do you really think, Mistress Burnett, that there's a place all brimstone flames to roast us sinners?"

She was startled by that difficult question, put to her so earnestly.

"I cannot tell; but I have heard that it is our own conscience which forms the fire."

Habbie reflected—thought of the toothache, rheumatism, and the agonies he had occasionally suffered after a "perfectly happy night." Then, drawing breath as if relieved—

" Oh, conscience ?—I think we can thole that."

He resumed his work. Beattie was placed in the hole, and the earth shovelled upon him. Habbie dug up some patches of moss and wild flowers, and planted them on the grave. He cut the name " Beattie " on the bole of the fir-tree, and his task was done.

Teenie was sitting on the trunk of a tree which had been blown down by the storm, the torn roots rising above her, and twisted into fantastic forms. She followed Habbie's movements with a sort of mechanical interest, all the time her mind was full of confused visions of Walter, her father, Baby, the Laird, the home she had left, and the unknown homeless future toward which she was moving. She wondered why she remained there when she wished to go on—anywhere so that she might lose herself if she could not find her father. She felt so very weak, and those pitiful commonplaces of life—the necessity of food, the want of money—so interfered with the grand sacrifice she desired to make, and turned all her efforts into the most prosaic failures.

She had the most disagreeable of all feelings—that she had been, and was, exceedingly foolish. What noble ends we might achieve if we were not fettered by the unconquerable conditions of nature! She felt cold, and yet hands and face were burning; the cheeks seemed aflame, and yet she was white as snow. The desire to go on with the sacrifice she had begun was strong and fierce; yet when she rose to quit the place, she felt as if she could not stand.

Habbie caught her arm, and supported her.

" You're no fit to go to Aberdeen, mem, your lane. Come back with me to Rowanden."

She struggled against the thought; but she was incapable of resistance, and he was quietly firm. He led her gently down by the cotter-houses, where he left the spade; then

8—2

on to the nearest station, where they had to wait a long time for the train. She shrank and quivered with shame at the idea of going home in this helpless state, with the knowledge that all her grand schemes had been frustrated, that she had inflicted much suffering upon herself, and perhaps upon others, without any result.

She would have run away from Habbie, but he kept close watch ; for although he had left Rowanden before her disappearance had become generally known, he had shrewd suspicions that there was something wrong, and in any case he had no doubt that home was the best place for her in her present state.

She tried several times to explain everything to this simple friend, and seek his help; but the words stuck in her throat and she could not utter them.

The train came at last, and they were carried to Rowanden. Instinctively Habbie conducted her from the station by the least frequented path. Weary and footsore she was guided up the hill by the poor poet, whose own heart was heavy enough, and yet he was able to feel for others, and to give kindly service.

The night was darkening as they ascended towards the manse. She hung back often, and he waited patiently. How would Walter receive her? He would turn her from his door as one unworthy to rest beneath his roof. He must scorn and hate her now; and she had failed so utterly in what she meant to do that she deserved his scorn.

She stopped, and wished to go on to the Norlan' Head, and obtain shelter from Ailie, who would forgive her anything. But Habbie said, No; home was the best place, and they were much nearer to the manse than to the Norlan' Head.

Home—home was the word he kept repeating; and unconsciously it influenced her steps. Yet she trembled with fear at thought of meeting the man she loved;

she shuddered in anticipation of his wrath.

The tramp of a horse's hoofs behind them! Glancing back they saw through the dusk a horseman slowly ascending the hill.

She drew quickly to one side into a gap in the hedge, and, dragging Habbie by the sleeve after her, she crouched down; Habbie made a pretence of trying to hide too, just to please her, but he was really wishing to be discovered.

The man rode by without seeing them, head bowed on his breast as if in despair, the horse dragging its legs as if utterly worn out.

It was Walter: she knew him. Two steps forward, and she could have touched him. Her heart swelled and throbbed like a wild bird, newly caged, beating itself against the bars of its prison, frenzied with fright and pain. Just to see him again—just to touch him—to kiss his hand—to whisper one imploring word, that might induce him to try to understand her—and then, she thought, it would be so sweet to lie down and rest, and to allow all this fever of mind and body to pass quietly away from her.

But he rode on ; she did not move and he did not see her. Then she trembled with sobs which supplied no relieving tears.

Another weary day of seeking without result, until man and horse were ready to drop with fatigue. He would have gone on himself until he had dropped, but he was merciful to the horse. The burden of his thought was still the same—" She will come back ; she will come back ;" and so, like a moth to the candle, he hovered about their home, hoping to find there the tidings of the wanderer which all his journeys failed to obtain.

He dismounted at the gate of the field behind the manse, took off the saddle and bridle, and turned the horse into the meadow.

Ailie met him as he entered the house.
She saw that he had no news, and did not
speak.   She relieved him of the harness, and
as she was doing so, he asked—

" Has there been any message for me ?"

" Never a word."

" My father has not been here ?"

" No."

He passed into his room.


Habbie waited for his companion to speak,
but he had to break the silence himself.
Touching her arm he said—

" Did you see yon, mistress ?"

" I saw—oh, but he looked wae, wae, and
I cannot go back !"

" Why no ?   When he's wae, that's just
the time he needs you ; and I'se warrant he's
been toiling himself to death seeking you.
Come, mem, let's go up to the house.   You
need rest, and there's nae place like hame, ye
ken."

She wished to go—she wished to be near

him, and yet she shrank back, dreading his scorn. The poet took her hand. She trembled, but did not draw back. Baby's cry seemed to ring in her ears again. Her heart was bursting with home-longings, and, unresisting, she was led up the hill to the gate. There she faltered again; but Habbie opened the gate, and gently drew her in.

Then a kind of fierceness rose within her. She expected to see the door closed in her face; to encounter pitiless disdain from him; and the passionate nature asserted itself; she was ready to be defiant and as scornful as he could be.

But the door stood wide open. So it had remained, by Walter's orders, night and day since her departure. There was a strange silence in the house—the silence which is in a house where some loved one lies dead.

Habbie drew her into the lobby, which was almost dark in the late gloaming. She yielded to him in her angry spirit more readily than she had done in her fear. She felt like one committed to a desperate adven· ture, and prepared to go on because turning back is impossible.

He glanced into the minister's room—the door of it was also open—and he whispered to her as he thrust her forward—

" He's there."

She saw him standing on the hearth, his arms crossed on the mantelpiece, and his head bowed on them. He heard the whisper, and the rustle of her dress, and turned round.

In the dim light each could just distinguish the form of the other. She was prepared to hear his bitter reproaches, and she stood, trembling, yet like one waiting for an enemy's attack. But he opened his arms, and said, in such a low tender voice—

" I knew you would come home, Teenie. Thank God !"

One big heart-bursting sob, and she would have fallen, but his arms were round her, and she was lying on his breast—new strength, new life thrilling through her veins in the knowledge of his love. Yet the new strength made her shame the greater ; scorn she could have met with scorn, but love humbled her. She could not look at him ; she could not speak to him ; all was so different from what she had anticipated, that she could only cling to him, hiding her face, and sobbing in the ecstasy of relief and shame. There are certain still moments which are pervaded by a sense of eternity, and love made this one of them to husband and wife. Their union was more perfect at this moment than it had ever been before.

# CHAPTER IX.

ABBIE retired to the kitchen as soon as he had seen Teenie safely into the room, and heard Walter's welcome to her. He found Ailie knitting in a vicious way, as if to keep herself from thinking, and Lizzie putting things to rights for the night. On his appearance, Ailie's first thought was to ask him if he had seen anything of the runaway. She thought of nothing else, indeed, except to lament her age and inability to trudge through the country in pursuit of Teenie. But here was the very man who was most likely to find her, if anybody could.

" If you'll give me something to eat, and promise that you'll no stir a foot from here till the minister comes, I'll tell you a' that you want to ken," he said, grinning to himself.

Ailie supplied him hastily with scones, cheese, and milk; and whilst he ate and drank he supplied her with all sorts of information except that which she desired most to have. When at last he told her, she would have rushed off to satisfy herself that he had spoken truth; but he held her back, and begged her to leave the minister and the guidwife to themselves for a little while. Ailie was convinced of his truth, and although she was full of anxiety to see her bairn again, she discreetly sat down, and resumed her knitting-needles. But the " wyving " process went on in a jerky, impatient fashion, and her only relief was to explain to Habbie, so far as she understood them, the details of Teenie's disappearance. Habbie narrated, with some embellishments, how he had met " the mistress," and how she looked so sickly that he had persuaded her to come home. Lizzie, wiping up dishes, listened with mouth wide open, and had to be frequently called to attention to her work by Ailie.

So the two were left uninterrupted.

They remained a long time without a word passing between them—he too happy to utter a word, she too full of joy and remorse to speak. He asked her no questions—he treated her as if she had been rescued from some great sickness or peril, and he was too glad to find her safe, to think of scolding her for having wilfully thrown herself into danger.

She did not feel irritated with him now for his quiet ways, or for treating her like a child. She was conscious of the love which kept him silent, and grateful for the trust of which all this was the proof.

"You are weary," he said by-and-by, "come and rest."

His arm supporting her fondly, they went upstairs. Baby was in his crib, a candle burning by his side, asleep with a bonnie smile on his fresh healthy face.

She dropped on her knees beside the crib, aud buried her face in the clothes. Then she fondled the child, timidly, fearing to wake him, and feeling that she was unworthy to touch him.

" My bairn, my bonnie bairn," she sobbed, " will you forgive me, as he has done ? Oh, but I've missed you, and the thought of you has been like the hand of God leading me home."

Walter stooped and raised her head. He passed his hand across her brow, trying to soothe her.

" My poor wifie, you have been much tried. But come, you will rest now, and we shall be very happy again when you have got the better of your fatigue."

" Don't, don't, Wattie—you make me feel wild, and ready to run away again. I wish I had never come back—I wish I had never been born."

" Hush !—I have been waiting for you. I knew that you would come back, and I'll try, Teenie, I'll try very hard to make your home a happy one. I shall hide every trouble from you, and show you nothing but the bright side of our life."

" That's just what I don't like. Oh, Wattie, make me part of yourself—tell me your sorrow as well as your joy, and that will content me. But you've tried to hide things from me, and that vexed me; it made me think you could not trust me as—as—you trust Grace."

There was no bitterness or jealousy in that cry, only the piteous appeal of one yearning to be helpful, eager to share his pain as well as his joy—the cry of a fond heart craving leave to prove its devotion.

A mist seemed to rise slowly from his vision ; he began to understand many things which had been hidden from him till now. He had regarded her too much as a creature of sunshine, and in his anxiety to divert all

shadows from her he had inflicted the deepest
sorrow.

" I have wronged you, Teenie—forgive
me."

At that she stared, wondering if he were
angry with her—it was so strange that he
should be asking forgiveness from her who
so much needed his. He was in sad earnest,
and she wondered the more. There was
such a buzzing in her head that she found it
difficult to recall the past or to realize the
present. She was home again—that was all
she knew; she was beside him and Baby—
that was all she cared for.

Timidly, as if still half afraid of a repulse,
she reached up her arms and clasped them
round his neck ; he, seating himself on a chair,
drew her upon his knee, and at that she clung
to him as if drowning, and he had come to
her rescue. She was ready to cry again for
joy.

" You never wronged me, Wattie ; you

have been always good, and kind, and true—
and, oh, I have been that wicked !"

" My darling—we must not speak of these
things now ; I want you to rest."

But she would not move ; she seemed afraid
to unclasp her hands lest this should prove to
be only another of the feverish dreams of
home which had visited her during that weary
aimless journey, and that she would waken
and find herself again on the desolate road,
friendless.

He saw that she was in a high state of excitement, and endeavoured to soothe her by
loving words and caresses, whilst he avoided
conversation.

Her eyes were fixed upon his face, eagerly
scanning every feature, noting every change
of expression ; it seemed to her as if she could
never look enough. By-and-by she spoke
again, in a low sobbing voice :—

" And I blamed you, Wattie—fancy that !
I thought you looked upon me as the cause

of all your misfortune, and that drove me wild because I felt it was true."

He tried to interrupt her with a kiss.

" Let me speak ; let me speak," she cried. " I was ready to do anything to serve you. I thought you would be happy if it was not for me, and so I went away, meaning to hide myself, and never come back. But you see I could not do that. I heard our bairn greeting, and I heard you crying to me wherever I went; and so my heart drew me home again, although my wish was to be far away. Are you .glad that I am here ?"

She put the question with tremulous earnestness, and he drew her closer to his bosom.

" There is nothing more needed for happiness than just to feel you are safe in my arms. We fret and worry over things that are lost, and never take account of the blessings that remain to us, until they too are swept away."

" And you would not like to lose me ?" she

said, fondling him, and, like a child that has been promised a new toy, she was eager to be told of his love over and over again.

" You know that I would not."

" Yes, I know now," she said, with a long-drawn sigh, for which there was no perceptible reason.

" Then I am going to be very stern with you now" (she looked frightened, and he smiled ; this was so unlike the Teenie who used to tease and defy him) ; " you shall find that I have become a great tyrant, and you must obey my slightest nod."

" I'll do everything you bid me," she said very humbly.

" Then I am going downstairs to get you something to eat and drink, and by the time I return you must be in bed."

" I don't want anything. Don't leave me."

He shook his head, pretending to frown, and she released him.

"Now remember : five minutes, and you are to be in bed."

He went quietly downstairs.

She pinched her arm, to see if she were awake. She could not yet believe that she was at home, in her own room ; Baby lying sound asleep in his crib beside her; and Walter unchanged, unless it might be that he was gentler with her than he had been of late. Yet she had been away three days, and he had asked her nothing, he had not scolded her, he had not breathed a word of blame, he had scarcely even alluded to her escapade. It was very bewildering to her.

She did not know the fierce struggle with passion through which the man had passed. She could not divine his brave resolve that he would win her back by love, to share in his attempt to reach that ideal life which he had imagined for them both.

Walter entered the kitchen so quietly that he startled two of its occupants ; the third, Lizzie, was fast asleep, sitting on a low chair,

her ruddy cheek pressed against the black
jamb of the fireplace.

He held up his finger, warning Ailie and
Habbie to speak low.

"You cannot see her to-night, Ailie," he
said in a whisper; "but you shall in the
morning, and then I want you to speak to
her as if she had never been away from
home. Ask her no questions, and do not
let her talk to you of the past three days.
Keep Lizzie downstairs. Now, get me
something to take up to her."

"Is she weel enough, sir, think you?"

"I cannot tell yet; she is greatly excited
and fatigued."

"Habbie thought she was kind o' fevered."

"The excitement would do that. Where
did you see her, Habbie?"

"She came home with me, sir."

"With you?"

"Ay;" and he rapidly told how he had
met Teenie.

Walter grasped the poet's hand, pressing it

gratefully. Kindness is a sort of telegraph; it brings the most distant social spheres into close communication one with the other.

" I'm thankful to have been able to do anything for you and the mistress, sir. I hope she'll be quite weel in the morning again," said Habbie—adding with a wry face, as if he had experienced the worst spite of fortune— " I care for little now, Beattie's dead."

Walter sympathized with him, and promised that he should have another Beattie.

" That's no possible, sir; I may get another donkey, but never another Beattie. But I'm obleeged to you, sir, all the same."

It was arranged that Habbie should obtain a gig at the inn, and carry the good news of Teenie's return to the Laird, and to Miss Wishart.

Walter took the tray which Ailie had provided, and went upstairs again.

Teenie had obeyed him ; she was in bed ; but her eyes were fixed upon the door, eagerly watching for him, and her face brightened at the first sound of his step on the stairs. She ate and drank because he wished her to do so, and because he was sitting beside her, holding the tray, and trying to tempt her by carving tit-bits of a chicken for her. Although the food seemed to sicken her, she took it to please him. At last the tray was removed to the table, and he sat down again beside her. She held his hand in both hers, as if she were afraid that he would leave her, and she kept her eyes upon his face with such fond yearning in them as shines on a lover's face on the eve of a long separation.

She tried to show her happiness and gratitude in smiles, since he objected to her speaking; but the smiles were not successful, they were too full of sad regret. He had spoken no word of reproach; he had given no hint of the vexation he must have endured on account of what she had done. How clear her vision was now! how plainly she saw the many ways in which she might have helped him, and in which she might help him still, please God! She had sought to redeem her error by one great sacrifice, and she had failed in that most ridiculously.

Now she began to see that it is in the trifles of life that help is needed most; in its great crises the nature of man or woman is strung up to hardihood, and is ready to stand or fall, as may be; but in the ordinary frets and cares of daily work, nature craves for sustaining sympathy. She was growing wise betimes : would it be too late ?

The love in his eyes reassured her ; there was time yet to redeem the past, and she meant to be very submissive. She was determined even to take charge of the Sunday-school, and of the winter charities. She was resolved to listen to his sermons and lectures without falling asleep !

He, too, was thinking of the many things left undone ; of the many ways in which he might have given her pleasure ; of the many ways in which he must have given her pain, by his unconscious neglect. He, too, was forming grand resolutions for the future.

At length her eyelids drooped, and she seemed to sleep; but by-and-by she wakened up, shuddering, and was only soothed by the pressure of his hand.

"You'll not guess what I've been thinking about," she said.

"I wish you would not think, but go to sleep."

"And you used to wish that I would think," she cried, laughing.

"Yes, but not when you are so tired as you are now."

"But I must tell you—it was awful. I thought the 'Christina' was a wreck, and that my father was drowned; was not that terrible?"

"Yes, but it was only a dream, and you once told me that dreams go by contraries. So we'll see the skipper home safe and merry as ever."

"Ay, but it could not be a dream, for I

was not asleep. It just came to me as I was thinking about everything; and then there came one of the verses of that old ballad I used to sing to him, and he liked so much— the verse that says—

> " ' And hey, Annie, and how Annie,
>     And Annie, winna you bide?'
> And aye the louder he cried Annie,
>     The braider grew the tide.

Was not that queer?"

" Not at all ; you have been thinking about your father; you are fatigued, and so dangers and nightmares come to disturb your mind. Now try to sleep."

" Put your arm round me then, and I'll try."

He placed his arm round her neck ; she rested her cheek upon it, and with a weary sigh she closed her eyes in sleep.

# CHAPTER X.

HE Laird was delighted by the news of Teenie's safe return to the manse, and he gave Habbie a crown-piece with thorough good-will. He had journeyed far and near in pursuit of her; he had telegraphed to everywhere within a circuit of thirty miles; he had fretted himself and exhausted himself in the vain pursuit, and he had returned that evening late, much tired and very hungry. He had often grumbled at the stupidity of detectives in failing to arrest criminals who had got the start of them: now that he had tried the detective business on a small scale, he pitied them.

He had dined; he was dozing in his easy-chair in the drawing-room whilst Alice read the "Times" to him, when Habbie arrived.

Of late Dalmahoy had been paying more than usual attention to public affairs; he was going earnestly into the question of the law of hypothec; he was zealously interested in regard to the repairs of farm-steadings, the erection of labourers' cottages, the abolishment of the bothy system, the drainage of land and the reclaiming of moorland; his interest in these matters became most intense just as he was about to cease to be a proprietor, and when he would have no opportunity of carrying out the grand schemes of amendment which occurred to him.

Miss Burnett was methodically manufacturing point-lace from a new pattern; Alice was reading sleepily, and marking every comma with a yawn, when Drysdale entered with the announcement that Habbie Gowk urgently desired to see the Laird.

"Confound the fellow! what does he want at this time of night?" grumbled Dalmahoy, stretching himself. " Did you finish that speech, Alice ?"

" I'm in the middle of the reply," she answered, hiding another yawn with the paper.

" Yes, yes, of course ; capital speech ; very clever; but the reply, so far as it has gone, promises to demolish it utterly."

"Why, it admits everything the speaker said."

" To be sure, child—we are always ready to admit everything we feel confident of being able to knock down. That's why I say it promises to demolish the argument."

He half rose from his chair, intending to see the visitor downstairs ; but he altered his mind, sat down again, and had Habbie brought into the drawing-room. The poet was not at all shy; he bowed to the ladies, and addressed himself to the Laird.

As soon as the message was delivered, Dalmahoy jumped up as nimbly as a youth.

"How funny!" exclaimed Miss Burnett, pausing with her needle half through a loop of the lace.

"I'm right glad to hear it," cried the Laird; "it's the blithest news that has come to me this long while; and Beattie shall have the biggest feed he ever had."

"Thank you, sir, thank you kindly, but ——Beattie's dead."

"Then you shall feed in his place," cried Dalmahoy, in his excitement forgetting the difference between man and beast.

The ladies smiled; Habbie saw nothing out of place, and gave his thanks quite sincerely. The Laird questioned him, and was still more delighted upon learning the details of the events. When Habbie had retired, he wiped his face with his bandanna, and thanked Heaven that there was one trouble the less to think about, as he resumed his seat.

"I do not see that her return under the escort of Mr. Gowk will at all relieve us of the scandal which her absence has caused," observed Miss Burnett, actuated by a severe sense of propriety.

"Confound the scandal, and the folk who deal in it!" muttered the Laird; "she's home and well, that's enough for us."

"But people will talk, papa, whether you are satisfied or not."

"Let them talk."

"You were not always so indifferent to what people said."

"There's no harm in growing wiser, Nelly, is there?"

"Oh no, if it be wiser to champion the cause of one who has disgraced the family."

"The family be —— just so; the family be happy: it has never done anything for me."

"Oh, papa!"

"Well, yes, I'm wrong: the family has done a great deal for me, and I have ruined it."

"You?"

" Yes, I have ruined it, and not Teenie ; blame me, not her."

" Why should we blame you ?" said Miss Burnett, rolling up her lace, and very much bewildered.

" Because I have spent the wealth of the family, and never made any for it."

" How funny !—excuse me, papa, the words came by accident ; but why did you not make wealth for the family ?"

The Laird drew himself up in his chair, feeling that he was put to the test.

" My dear, money-making is a special talent—I might say it is genius—just as money-spending is a misfortune. There are some men who toil like slaves, wear their hearts out struggling for money, who deny themselves everything, and yet never get their heads above water—they are for ever at the last gasp ; do what they will, strive as they will, they can never overcome the necessities of the moment. There are others— those who are endowed with the talent—who dash along, recklessly we might think, but they always land on their feet. They enjoy life, appear in purple and fine linen, and deny themselves nothing; in time they become millionaires or bankrupts; but they are quite happy either way. If millionaires, they go on enjoying themselves; if bankrupts, they begin again with better prospects than ever. I belong to the first class."

"But you could not help that, papa, you never were in trade."

"So much the worse for me—or rather for you. I have a profound admiration for trade, and really believe that I had some qualifications for it. The trader is the modern knight-errant: he helps the needy, he conquers kingdoms and populates deserts; he wages a perpetual crusade on the undeveloped resources of nature, and his adventures are none the less daring because they render practical service to humanity." ("Humph! capital that would have been for the agricultural dinner. Pity the best things always occur to me *after* my speech," he muttered to himself ; and then aloud), " I refer to this, my dears, because I am likely to begin business myself."

"You, papa !" exclaimed Alice, without yawning.

" How funny !" ejaculated Miss Burnett, closing the top of her dainty work-table, and locking it; " I can't imagine you beginning business at your age."                              •

" My dear, you have a happy way of supplying us with the most uncomfortable memoranda."

He got up and stood on the white Angola hearthrug, swinging his glasses meditatively.

" Age is honourable," he went on, " but youth is beautiful ; and most of us would be pleased to dispense with the honour in order to share in the beauty."

" I did not mean to offend you."

" Not the least offence in the world is imagined, my dear. But this business idea of mine is not a whim, it is a necessity."

" A necessity—how ?"

The Laird coughed and changed the subject.

" I wish we could discover some nice present to give Teenie," he said, as if his whole mind were devoted to the discovery.

Miss Burnett became prim immediately. She had not forgotten Walter's reception of her on Sunday, and she could not overlook the outrageous impropriety of Teenie's escapade.

" But I really cannot understand why Christina should be permitted to do with impunity what would be severely punished in others. She was admitted to a family of distinction, she was accepted as one of its members and made welcome. I think it was her *duty* to respect that family, and to suffer anything rather than bring disgrace upon it. I really cannot excuse her, papa, and I cannot understand how you are so lenient to her."

" Oh, Helen, you are too hard upon her !" cried Alice.

" You are such a giddy young thing, Alice,
that I forgive you. I am *not* hard upon
Christina, but she has been hard upon us.
Poor people who have been raised to a
position should remember the gratitude they
owe to those who have raised them. I pity
her, but I think that she ought to be made to
feel her action has been most reprehensible."

Alice shrank behind the " Times " at this
severe reproof, and ignominiously retired from
the defence of her sister-in-law.

" Don't talk of poor people, Helen ; or if
you do, talk of them with friendly feeling,"
said the Laird, with a long-drawn sigh ; " you
don't know how soon we may be reckoned
amongst them. I was telling you about that
business project of mine. I mean to take a
farm—I could manage a farm, I think—and
shall try all my new theories of drainage and
manuring in a practical manner. I mean to
work with my own hands."

" Oh, that will be delightful, papa !" cried
Alice ; " and I'll learn to milk the cows, and

I'll get such a pretty milkmaid's dress; and
you shall learn to sing, 'Of a' the joys of earth
that the tongue of man can name, is to woo
a bonnie lassie when the kye comes hame.'
It will be charming, and I'll enjoy it so much."

And so with that pretty picture of a pasto-
ral life, as represented in china ornaments,
Alice was eager to begin the business adventure of which the Laird had spoken. He
held out his hand, and she, though not accustomed to familiar endearments, jumped up,
put her arms round his neck, and called him
her "dear, young papa."

"Ha, ha, you rogue! you are ever so much
more sensible than that wise sister of yours."

Miss Burnett was quite indifferent to this
depreciation of her merits, and with an admirably practical view of affairs she observed—

"But why should you take a farm, papa?
Why should not this pretty experiment be
carried out at home?"

That pulled him up; he felt for a moment

spiteful enough to declare why he was compelled to think of this speculation, and to
humble Miss Burnett by showing her upon
what very thin ice she was standing. But
there was Alice in her pretty childish way
hanging round his neck, and forming such
sweet visions of a toy farmstead, that he could
not find it in his heart to dispel the dream.

" They'll learn the truth soon enough," was
his thought; "let them be happy in their
ways as long as they can. Why should I
disturb them? The time is so short when
they must know all and suffer."

So he put off the question with a jest, and
said good-night with even more good-humour
than usual.

"We cannot try it here, Helen, for several
reasons. We might spoil your butter by
new-fangled experiments; and in the strict
order of things we might find it necessary to
send your pet lamb to the flesher."

" Oh, fie, papa !" cried Alice; " you never
could do that."

"Necessity has no law; needs must when the—etc. Good-night, my dear, and pleasant dreams."

He kissed her, and turned to his eldest daughter, who rose and kissed him—an unusual display of affection, which made him hold her arms a minute, looking into her eyes curiously.

"I hope I haven't vexed you, papa, by anything I have said about Christina. I *will* try to think of her as you do, but I can't help feeling that she has been most foolish."

"We are all so foolish at times, my dear, that we are only wise when we pardon the folly of others. What would you say, now, if I told you that in consequence of my folly we would have to quit Dalmahoy—have to walk out penniless and homeless, with nothing to depend upon but what we could earn for ourselves? What would you say to that piece of folly?"

"What ridiculous things you do think about, papa!"

" Is that all you would say ?"

" How can I tell you in jest what I would say if you spoke in earnest ? I would be very unhappy, of course, but I would try to help you all the same, in whatever way you thought best."

" And you, Alice ?"

" I don't know, you dear, imaginative papa. I suppose I would say you had been very very foolish, and that I was angry with you, and that I would work day and night, and that I would love you more and more, because you were unhappy."

" My darlings"—and he embraced them both—" don't speak of the folly of others until you know what folly you have to excuse at home."

Then, with a hasty good-night, he went out of the room, took up his candle from the table in the hall, and went down to the library.

The two ladies regarded his abrupt departure with surprise, and then they looked at each other inquiringly.

"What *can* papa mean ?" exclaimed Alice, anxiously.

" He is only making fun of us," said Helen, composedly.

That was satisfactory, and the two retired for the night.

The Laird found his lamp burning low, and he turned it up. Although it was still early autumn, a fire was cheery in the evenings. He poked the fire, and settled down in his chair, without book or paper, apparently content to amuse himself with his own reflections, and the phantasms he might discover in the embers.

It was hard—much harder than he had anticipated—to give up the old life of position, and of comparative comfort, and to begin a new life of struggle and speculation at his years, as Helen had said. He had thought that he could meet it calmly, and, depending upon the innumerable schemes for attaining wealth which he had concocted, and which he had never carried out for want of capital, but which he would now be able to enter upon with other people's capital, since he had nothing of his own to lose, he had fancied that it would be an easy matter to retire from Dalmahoy, and to make a comfortable living for his children by the force of talent and industry. But it was not easy. Sentimental reasons aside—and these sentimental reasons assumed huge proportions as the day of doom approached—he found his confidence in his own powers rapidly decrease as the calamity became more imminent.

What was he to do with those children— he always thought of them as children, notwithstanding their years—who had learned nothing useful, and who were utterly unfitted to earn their own living? He blamed himself. He ought to have taught them something that would have been of practical value to them in such a crisis as the present. But who could have suspected such a crisis? That was no excuse. He ought to have been ready for it, and he was much to blame. *That* would not have mattered, only they had to suffer in consequence of his neglect.

Then there were strange shadows reaching out of the past, which added much to the bitterness of his position. He began to feel that his years were weighing very heavily upon him, and that the farce of youthfulness was played out.

" A man without money, without the vigour of youth, and with a family to feed and dress —what a helpless beggar he is ! I begin to appreciate the blessedness of the rest which is to be found in the kirk-yard—ugh ! how morbid I grow !"

He stirred the fire again, and found a sort of grim comfort in watching the old forms and faces which appeared to him in the embers. What duties he had neglected—and what a number of pleasures of which he had stupidly failed to take advantage! Night has a strange influence on the nerves.

# CHAPTER XI.

ALTER would have persuaded Teenie to keep her bed during the next day; but something of the old rebellious spirit showed itself already, and she prayed so hard to be permitted to go downstairs that, although he saw how excited she was still, and that she was quite feverish, he yielded. She kissed him and thanked him so gratefully, that he was glad he had yielded, notwithstanding his conviction that it was wrong.

She dressed with a sort of wild gaiety— like a child who has just been pardoned some offence for which severe punishment had been expected. But she watched him with eager eyes, wondering why he asked her nothing about her absence. Downstairs she met Ailie, who showed no surprise, no unusual delight at seeing her home again—spoke and acted just as if those weary wanderings of Saturday, Sunday, and Monday had never occurred.

Teenie felt puzzled and frightened by this silence. Had it been only a painful dream ? Or was this a plan to make her feel the more the punishment that was to come ? She would rather have had it all out at once, and yet it was pleasant to drop into the old routine of life as if there had been no break, no torture of fear and suspense to Walter, no frenzied effort on her part to save him by sacrificing herself.

But she had been very weak; she had begun a sacrifice which would have been of service to him, and she had utterly failed to carry it out. She winced terribly at that thought; she felt herself to be so weak and worthless—and yet it was so sweet to be near him again, to hear his voice, and feel his loving care for her as she had not felt it for many days, that she was almost glad at her failure.

The gaping mouth and staring eyes of Lizzie, when she brought in the tea-kettle, were sufficient proofs that the adventures of the past few days were real. The girl had been warned by Walter and threatened by Ailie with severe punishment if she forgot that she was not to say a word to her mistress; but neither warning nor threats could extinguish the amazement expressed on her countenance.

The feverish excitement of Teenie's manner seriously alarmed her husband, although he tried hard to be quietly cheerful. She would scarcely allow him to leave her for a moment, and she would not allow Baby to be taken from her on any account. She washed him and dressed him herself; she fed him and nursed him, although it was plain that she was sustained only by excitement which would break down suddenly. She wanted to show how strong she was, and that her wickedness had not injured her health, at any rate.

But Walter, as he saw the flushed face, and occasionally felt the dry hot hand, became more and more anxious about her, and more convinced that he ought to have insisted upon her remaining in bed.

The Laird came shortly after breakfast.

Teenie, who seemed to have eyes and ears for everything, was the first to be aware of his approach. She trembled; the blood rushed violently to her face, and then forsook it, leaving her cheeks white. She was almost as much afraid to encounter Dalmahoy as she had been to meet her husband.

Walter, observing these signs of agitation, proposed to speak to his father before admitting him; but she grasped his arm and held him back.

" No, Wattie," she said with apparent composure, " I would rather not have you begging mercy for me."

There was no time for discussion. Dalmahoy was already on the threshold of the room.
He was not so spruce this morning as usual ;
his face was not so fresh, his hair seemed to
have more white than formerly, and his shirt-
front was not so scrupulously smooth as it was
his custom to have it. There was, however,
a sly twinkle in his eyes when he observed
the position of husband and wife.

She had placed Baby in his basket, and he
was lying there crowing manfully, and trying
to swallow his fat, puffy fingers ; and she was
still standing in the act of restraining Walter
from going out to meet the Laird.

" So, madam," exclaimed the latter, sternly,
striding up to her, and clutching his riding-
whip as if he had some thoughts of using it,
" you have been trying to frighten us ; you
have neglected your duties as a wife and a
mother, and you have been disgracing our
family ! What have you to say for yourself ?"

" Father !" cried Walter, in utter amazement and horror at this address, for it entirely reversed the system by which he had
been trying to win Teenie back to peace and
content.

She had been trembling with timidity at
his entrance, remembering the tenderness he
had shown her in their last interview at
Dalmahoy; but this grim address completely
changed her—she became doubly defiant.
Love could lead her anywhere, make her do
anything; but sound a harsh note, and strong
ropes could not draw her.

" It's none of your business what I have to
say for myself," she retorted fiercely.

" So that's your humour, is it ?   We must
tame this proud spirit, and——"

There was passion expressed by her
features, but there were bitter tears in her
eyes, and he paused.

She saw a tender father's smile growing
through the sorrow which was stamped on
his face ; she saw his arms open as if to re-

ceive her, and with a little joyful sob she
threw herself into them.

"God bless you, my child!" he said, and
his voice faltered slightly as he kissed her ;
" I did not think you would believe me in
earnest. I'm right glad to see you, my braw
lass, and I don't care a button what you have
to say for yourself, since you have had the good
sense to come back to us and relieve us,
though you have made my old bones ache
hunting after you."

" Did you seek me, then ?"

" Did we seek you !—my certes ! we have
been all over the country looking for you,
and how you escaped us is a puzzle to me.
But I blame that gowk of a man of yours for
everything."

She became fierce again, and withdrew
from his arms.

" But you must not blame him !" she cried ;
" he is true and brave, and I shall never be
able to love him enough for all his goodness
to me."

"Well, well! there's no accounting for tastes," grinned the Laird, quite wickedly; "as I've often said, he has capital ideas in his head sometimes, but they are like a midges' dance, so ravelt that you can make nothing of them."

"You must not say that; and I'll run away from you if you do."

"Well, I won't say it. Wattie understands me, and he'll take no offence. I dare say he is a good-enough sort of a chiel when you come to know him."

"I'm content to leave my character in your hands," said Walter, smiling; for he was very happy to see how Teenie had won the Laird entirely to her side.

Seeing that, he determined to obey a summons which he had received an hour before, and which was just then repeated urgently—to attend old Mr. Geddies, who wished to see him; he had only to cross the road, so he would be back soon. As he was going out, Baby began to assert his authority, and to call attention to himself by a vigorous and continued cry. Teenie lifted and soothed him by means of various tender arts and his feeder.

" I detest babies," said the Laird; "they are such stupid lumps of flesh and fibre, and they howl so. We ought to be all born grown up with a thousand a year."

At the same time Dalmahoy patted the chubby cheeks of Baby, and was vastly amused when the little fellow clutched one of his fingers, and crowed over it as a prize.

" How touzy your hair is to-day !" cried Teenie, laughing ; "and now I'll punish you for giving me such a scare when you came in —there, hold Baby till I come back."

She deposited her charge on his lap ; the Laird dropped his whip, called her back, and sat in much confusion at the absurd position he occupied. Baby began to cry again.

" The wee deevil," growled the Laird ; " can he not be quiet till she comes back ?"

Then to quiet Baby, he baa'd like a sheep,

cackled like a hen, crowed like a cock, and
imitated other animals, tickling and hoisting
his charge the while ; so that when Teenie
returned, she heard the child screaming with
delight—saw the Laird tossing him in the air
whilst he brayed like a donkey. He looked
shamefaced, and a little vexed, when he found
that he was observed ; then he laughed
heartily.

" 'Pon my soul, Teenie, you're a witch !" he
exclaimed, "and you make a fool of me just
as you please. Here, take your confounded
bairn—he's a nuisance."

" No, keep him till I dress your hair. He's
very happy, and laughing as if he had the
best nurse in the world."

Baby screeched with delight as the Laird
tickled him, crying, " Chucky, chucky,
chuck—y !" and uttered other nonsensical
sounds which represent baby-language. She
combed and brushed his hair, drawing back
now and again to study the effect of her
arrangements with the eye of an artist.

Finally, whilst he still nursed Baby, she drew him to a mirror to look at himself.

" There !" she cried proudly, " isn't that better ?"

"Wonderful !" he exclaimed, putting up one hand to arrange a curl at the side of his head, " ten years knocked off the account. I'd kiss you if my hands were released from this bundle."

So he placed the bundle in its basket, and he took her hands, and touched her brow with his lips. He became serious at that moment.

" You have made me young again, my child ; but why are you so hot and feverish ?"

He now observed how strange she looked ; there was a wild restlessness in the eyes, and a quivering of the lips, which at first might have been attributed to her agitation and doubt as to the reception she was to have, but could not be explained by these suggestions any longer since they were friends re-united. Her whole frame seemed to be on fire, and yet she was shivering ; that startled him.

"I don't know what is the reason—I'm queer," she answered hurriedly, and flying away to the subject which was uppermost in her thoughts—"but what about Dalmahoy ?"

He gave his shoulders an uncomfortable twist.

"There's nothing new about it," he said with a grin ; "there will be letters of horning issued against me soon, I suppose."

"What's that horning ?"

"Only a summons in the name of Her Majesty the Queen (God bless her), commanding me to pay the siller forthwith or—get out."

"And you say that as quietly as if it was the ruin of somebody else you were talking about !" she said wonderingly.

"Just that ; it's surprising how easily we can bear our neighbours' burdens ; so I try to think that it is not me, but another fool, who is about be turned out in his old age to learn how to gain a decent living."

He spoke gaily enough, but there was a rueful shadow in his eyes. Then she, with a voice that was full of pain—

" I wish I had never come back—I wish I had died by the roadside, and I would have been happy, looking down upon you all."

" You would have seen us miserable beggars when you were away from us, Teenie."

" No, no, you would have been safe and comfortable—I went away thinking that Mistress Wishart would give you the money if she only knew me to be out of the road. But I've come back and spoiled it all."

Walter was at the door, and heard her. He understood everything now—the idea of self-sacrifice which had possessed her, and which he reverenced none the less that it appeared to him a foolish one, and he understood the bitterness of heart which she experienced in her failure. He knew something of the bitterness of failure, and he loved her more and more, if that could be. He embraced her tenderly.

"My poor wifie, you must not agitate yourself in this way," he said affectionately ; "you must not take all our sins upon yourself. Come, be cheerful, Teenie, I have splendid news for you."

"Has the cow calved twins?" said the Laird, laughing, and yet with a kind of girn in the laugh, as if he found it difficult to be cheerful under the circumstances.

Walter's touch revived her, and she looked at him for explanation.

"Better than that, sir; old Geddies sent for me to say that he has determined to resign the church and all its emoluments to me."

"That's four or five hundred a year at least," ejaculated Dalmahoy ; "I congratulate you, Wattie—and myself, for now I'll be able to borrow from you."

"Will it save Dalmahoy?" was Teenie's question.

Walter was unable to answer, but the Laird took up the matter.

"You must get Dalmahoy out of your head,

Teenie," he said quite blithely ; " we'll manage to live without it. Wattie's luck will
make you comfortable here, but it can do
nothing up the way."

" Unless we could obtain a loan on the
strength of this income," suggested Walter.

" Fiddlesticks ! we'll try nothing of the
kind. We'll keep what we've got, and make
the best of it. I'm as blithe as a peacock with
a new tail spread out, Wattie ; but if I let you
sink your good fortune in the whirlpool öf
mine, may I be——All right, Teenie, I was
not going to swear."

Peter Drysdale, on urgent business, was an-
nounced by Ailie. The old butler entered
eagerly.

" You bade me bring any letters direct after
you, sir, and as you were anxious, I came on
with this myself."

The Laird read the letter, and quietly re-
folded it.

" It's all over, Wattie ; I have humbled myself and asked this scoundrel for time to pay.

He refuses—says he is pressed for money himself, and that the debt is so long owing I ought to be ready to redeem it now. So up go the bills for the sale. Now then, gentlemen, here's a fine property, and a d——d ass of an old man—going, going—gone!"

# CHAPTER XII

DALMAHOY spoke with a sort of forced levity, but he displayed much more agitation than his son had ever witnessed in his manner before.

" It will be fine fun for our neighbours, and they will show marvellous wisdom in descanting upon my ruin," he went on, with a half-bitter, half-humorous grin ; "throughout the nine days' wonder you will hear them crying, ' Serve him right—what a scamp he was in his young days !—what a wastrail !' and so on, and so on. The worst of it—or the best of it, I am not sure which—is that it's all true. Well, sowing wild oats was very nice —for me, and I won't say a word about that; but they produce a confoundedly nasty crop for those who come after me, and that's disagreeable to think about. Good-bye—come over this evening, if you can ; I would like to have a chat with you, and ask your advice about the arrangement of things for the sale.  I must hurry off now to write some letters, and to meet the architect, who is to show me a plan for the improvement of the steadings on the estate.  I don't think it will all go ; but we'll see.  Where's Teenie ?"

She had become very quiet ; she heard every word that was said, but she was bending over Baby's basket, pretending to be deeply occupied, although healthy and ignorant little Hugh was fast asleep.  The crisis had come at last, and her pulses were beating wildly ; the pitiless words of Dame Wishart were ringing in her ears, making them burn with pain and shame ; and the thought that she alone was accountable for all this misfortune—that but for her there would have been no difficulty in arranging the Laird's

affairs—maddened her. There was no news
of Skipper Dan yet.

She rose up when Dalmahoy asked for
her, and he took her hands kindly.

" You are very feverish, my child ; you
must take care of yourself for all our sakes
—God bless you—good-bye."

" Good-bye," she answered, with a curiously
trembling voice, and suddenly she put her
arms round his neck, kissed him, and ran
out of the room.

" That's fine, Teenie ; come back and do
it again," he cried quite gaily ; adding, with
much satisfaction, " On my soul, Wattie, I
feel the better of it."

Every sympathetic word or look supplies
an appreciable quantity of nerve-force, and
helps a man more than pounds of money  It
is so much courage, and therefore so much
strength, to a man with the least sincerity in
his nature. That was the Laird's experience
at this moment.

Walter accompanied him to the gate, where

his horse was tied. As he was putting his foot in the stirrup—

" There was a time, Wattie, when I might have been grumbling at you for this; but I see now it's my own fault and my own ill-luck. You were right to marry Teenie; she's a fine creature, and I'm fond of her. Be good to her, and she'll make you happy. As for me, I have been selfish, therefore a fool, and I am punished."

" I too have been selfish and thoughtless— which is the worse sin ?" muttered Walter.

" I don't know, and it doesn't matter," was the answer as he settled himself in the saddle ; " but next time you preach, take that text about being sure your sins will find you out —is it a text or a tract ? My sins have found me out at any rate, or rather they have caught me at home, and they are using the lash without mercy. I'll tell you a secret—but don't be too hard on me, Wattie : we are none of us pretty under the microscope, and poverty is about the most unsparing microscope I ever heard tell of. That fellow, Geordie Methven, was my son, and there he has left a million which nobody is likely to get the least good of, and here am I, his father, about to be made a beggar for want of a few thousands. It's hard lines, take it how you will. Good-bye—take care of Teenie—she's not well."

He rode away without giving Walter time for reply. The revelation was startling enough, but scarcely so startling as it would have been had not Walter, at various periods, heard faint rumours of the paternity of George Methven. The case did seem a hard one, and, minister though he was, he pitied rather than blamed his father. At the same time he experienced a sharp pang at the thought that Methven should have been capable of amassing wealth which would have relieved their father of all trouble, whilst he seemed to be scarcely capable of struggling above poverty.

He pulled himself up at that; he had adopted a career which was full of possibilities for serving others; he was bound in honour to accept all its responsibilities and difficulties with brave steadiness of heart, and he would do so—please God.

A quiet nature, full of devotion to religion, and to the practical expression of it by helping all, so far as in him lay, by blaming none —that was Walter. He was capable of pitying the most atrocious criminal; he was so conscious of weakness in himself that he was sorry for the errors of others, and whilst he condemned the sins, he was merciful to the sinners. Always he argued, " Under the same circumstances, I might have acted like them." And so he was kind, gentle, and helpful to the backslider, because he pitied and sympathized with him or her.

He attended the funerals of Red Sandy, Buckie Willie, and of other unfortunate fishers who had perished in the recent storm, and whose bodies had been recovered from the sea. The entire male population of Rowanden paid the last mark of respect to their dead

comrades ; the women kept indoors, as according to custom, they were not permitted
to proceed to the churchyard.

From the top of the hill the procession
looked like a long dark line curving to the
bends of the road, and moving with slow
solemnity up the hill towards the church.
Most of the men were dressed in black suits,
all in black coats. The coffins were con-
veyed in carts the greater part of the way ;
but when near the church they were taken
upon the shoulders of stalwart fishermen, the
carts drawing to one side, to permit the procession to pass. All spoke in undertones,
as if they were afraid of disturbing the repose of the dead. The conversation generally related to the deceased friends ; their
many good and kindly qualities were affectionately remembered; all their faults were forgotten. But there were also occasional refer-
ences to the state of the weather and the
prospects of the next night's fishing.

It was a bleak day; there had been rain,

the grass was heavily wet ; and the " Razor "
was blowing keenly over the land, compelling
the mourners to put up their hands to their
hats, tossing their hair, and flapping the tails
of their coats.

There were a number of gigs and other
vehicles following in the wake of the procession — farmers, extensive fish - curers, and
others, from Kingshaven, amongst whom was
the provost, five proprietors who had to attend a meeting of heritors, and Mr. Forsyth,
banker, lawyer, and factor to Sir James Scott,
the patron of Rowanden Kirk. Mr. Forsyth
had been summoned by the old minister, Mr.
Geddies, in regard to the latter's proposed
resignation.

The burial over, the fishers returned to the
village, and enjoyed a holiday. There was
mourning for a little while, and many regrets
for those who were lost. But work must be
done : the mourning was soon over ; women
gathered bait and men went out to the fishing
just as usual—laughed and made merry when

they were in luck, and grumbled when they
were out of it. There is a merciful buoyancy
in human nature, and ordinary sorrow, as well
as ordinary joy, only touches the heart and is
gone.

Walter had several unpleasant experiences
to endure this day, and he had need of all his
patience. He had to listen to some severe
reflections upon himself—he could bear that :
but he had also to listen to disagreeable reflections upon his wife, offered to him in the
form of condolence, and that he could not
bear. To the surprise of everybody he de-
fended Teenie with a vehemence which he
had not previously displayed out of the pulpit.
He would not permit one word to be said in
her dispraise; they might say what they
pleased about himself, and he was mute ; but
touch her name, and he was up in arms, fierce
as a raging lion.

Mr. Pettigrew, with his partiality for unpleasant truths (and possibly with some recol-
lection of the way in which the young minis-

ter had snubbed him on various occasions), was the first to hint that, as an elder, he could not possibly give his sanction to the appointment of Mr. Burnett as the successor of the much-respected Mr. Geddies, until certain scandals connected with his household were investigated by the presbytery, and satisfactorily explained to them.

Walter writhed under this vulgar publicity of his household troubles, and his first impulse was to refuse the appointment altogether; but that would be to cast a doubt upon his faith in Teenie, and so he said quietly that he would not permit Mr. Pettigrew, or any one else, to interfere with his private affairs. It was torture to him to speak in this way, for he felt how weak it was without explanations, which he could not give even to friends, and which he would not give in the presence of such a man as Pettigrew. Then again came the thought to turn away at once from the thankless task he had undertaken; and that suggestion was met by the resolve to hold his place, even for her sake, and to defend her honour by showing his own faith in her. But it is easier to spoil a good impression than to erase a bad one, and he had much to endure for days afterwards. People looked at him askance, whispered about his affairs, pitied him; and a few members of his congregation (those who had declared he was not "sound" after his defence of the poor woman who had been charged with selling sweeties on the Sabbath) openly expressed their disapproval of Mrs. Burnett's conduct, and of the minister's in defending her.

It was hard to bear, but he did not flinch or falter. His chief anxiety was to keep the scandal from Teenie's ears ; and in this desire he was successful, but the source of his success was a sad one.

On reaching home after the harassing work of the day, Ailie told him that Teenie had gone to Craigburn.

" To Craigburn—what for ?" he exclaimed.

" I canna say, but she got Drysdale to take her in the gig."

" Did my father know ?"

" He was away before she started."

Walter had no difficulty in guessing the object of her journey; and, worn out by the events and discussions of the forenoon, he felt irritated with her for going to see his aunt without consulting him. Frowning, he put on his hat again, took his staff, and went out to meet her.

# CHAPTER XIII.

HAT time when she became so quiet, Teenie had devised a scheme by which she might yet help Dalmahoy and Walter. The hope was very faint—the execution of the scheme demanded the sacrifice of every remnant of pride which still lingered in her breast. But her nervous excitement had attained such a pitch that she seemed to have strength for the most desperate adventure.

Drysdale, who had much liking for her, readily agreed to stay behind the Laird, and to drive her to Craigburn. Arrived at the door, she found it open. Pate was lying on the mat, and saluted her with a kindly wag of his tail. There was no one about, but there were sounds of laughing voices in the kitchen regions. Teenie marched straight in and up the stairs to the door of Dame Wishart's room. She paused an instant. What was she going to say or do ? Impulse had carried her thus far ; on the road, eagerness to be at the place, and fear of her own resolution failing, rendered her incapable of forming any plan of action. The dame had inspired her with a certain awe, and, if she allowed herself to think about it, she dreaded the possibility of being frightened away without accomplishing her purpose.

With feverish haste she turned the handle of the door, and so committed herself beyond the possibility of retiring.

On the instant she seemed to become unnaturally cold and calm ; now that there was no retreat, fear was banished. Her eyes and brain became clear ; she saw everything, understood everything, and yet she felt as if her soul were standing aside, watching her

body going through the scene which followed.

Grace was sitting near the window, sewing ;
Dame Wishart sat in her big chair, leaning
back on the soft cushions, apparently sleeping.
Grace turned at the opening of the door, gave
a little start of surprise at seeing Teenie, and,
finger on lips as if to beg silence, advanced
quickly.   She embraced her affectionately.

" Come   down   stairs," she whispered,
" where we can speak without disturbing my
mother."

" I came to beg of you," said Teenie, in a
low voice.

" What ?"

" To let me speak to your mother alone.
It is for Walter's sake, and the Laird's."

Grace looked at her, and divined her intention ; but she did not like the excited brightness of her eyes.

" Go in," she said ; " I'll help you if I can."

She passed out, closing the door gently
after her.

Teenie stepped forward, and stood beside the big chair. The dame's head was thrown back—the eyes still remained closed. The large features, wrinkled and sallow, were like those of a strong man whom the hand of Death has touched. A hard unyielding face, and yet now in its repose there were lines of suffering scored upon it which commanded sympathy, if not affection.

Strange caprice—the face reminded her of her father's; all that the dame had done on account of Grace, he would have done on her account. Impulsively she stooped and kissed the withered lips.

" Aye, aye, Grace—you thought I was sleeping, my doo, but you're mistaken; I've been watching you," muttered the dame.

She slowly opened her eyes upon the stranger ; she glanced at the seat her daughter had just vacated, then at Teenie.

" Who are you ?"

Teenie was calm and resolute as the dame herself now.

" I used to be called Teenie Thorston ; Burnett is my name now."

Dame Wishart stared at her for a minute in silence ; then, impatiently—

" What do you want ?"

" Your help—money."

" What for ?"

" Dalmahoy."

Surprised as she was by this singular attack, and puzzled as she was by the unaccountable absence of Grace, the dame, having somewhat of the Laird's sense of humour, was amused by the sharpness and directness of the replies. But she still regarded the visitor with a frowning brow, and the thin lips tightly drawn. There was a kind of sarcastic indifference in her tone.

" Aye, lass, you've a glib tongue in your head—who put you up to it ?"

" To what ?"

" To come here—who sent you ?"

" No one."

"My certes, then you're not blate to come to me without leave asked. You are no friend of mine."

"I know that," she said simply, and her heart seemed to swell with a sob which she had difficulty in suppressing; the effort threatened to upset all her resolution.

Harsh and stern to her as Dame Wishart was, Teenie's heart was yearning so for a kind word, a kind look, that she could have loved the old lady tenderly if she would have given her leave.

"Then what right have you to come to me with such demands?"

The dame reached out her hand to touch the bell which stood on a little table by her side.

"I have no right," she said, and her voice was very pathetic in its submission; "only I wanted to speak to you, because there is nobody to save us but you. You have satisfied the Laird and Walter that there is no help to be got from you—they would be angry if

they knew what I was doing, but I do it because you have not satisfied me."

" Why not, since the others know me well
enough to take my word ?"

" Because I won't believe that your heart
is dead."

The dame started, withdrew her hand
from the bell, and allowed the arm to rest on
the table.

" The heart may be quick enough, and yet
seem cold when it is doing justice. What
else ?"

" Because you have a daughter who is
good, brave, and noble—who has sacrificed
her life to you—I cannot believe that you
are ready to make her ashamed of your
memory."

The dame looked at her sharply, lips
trembling a little. Then—

"You are a bold hussy—what do you
mean ?"

" I mean that in refusing to save your
brother from ruin you bring misery on us all,

and Grace will share it—she will feel it worse than any of us, for she will feel that you, her mother, have doomed her to a life of shame and regret."

" What shame or regret can there be to her ?"

" The shame of thinking that you, because you could not force a man to marry her, revenged yourself upon those who were blameless in order to reach him."

The cold stern eyes were fixed on her face; hard and pitiless sounded the voice.

" Did you come here to preach—to me ?"

" No; to beg."

But with these words all Teenie's courage evaporated; the woman seemed so immovable, cold and hard as a rock; she seemed to have vexed her rather than persuaded her— seemed to have rendered her more resolute than ever not to give the needed assistance. Teenie made another effort to control herself, to remain calm and . firm ; but her body swayed to and fro, she seemed to stagger and then she dropped down at the dame's feet.

" Ah, madam, I cannot speak right—I am like a child. I spoke just now thinking to frighten you, and trying to hide from you the pain that I am suffering. But what I said is true, although I cannot hide my pain. I wanted to persuade you to act for their sakes as if I had no share in their joy or sorrow ; and now I can only cry to you—think of them, and forget me."

Teenie's piteous appeal did not appear to have more effect than her bold argument. The dame remained silent, looking at her, and yet the eyes seemed to be seeking something beyond the kneeling figure. There had been things said which had already suggested themselves to her mind, and stirred disagreeable sensations. She could be unforgiving to everybody except Grace. On her account she was ready to do much that was opposed to her own humour.

Imprisoned for many years in this room by

physical ailment—although comforted by the happy hallucination that the disablement was only temporary, and that she would soon be up and doing with all the brisk activity of early days, and resolutely shutting her eyes to the lapse of time until she became really insensible to it—the dame's sympathies had become narrow as her life. She saw nothing to care for, felt there was nothing worth caring for, beyond Grace, her constant companion and nurse.

Yet she had quick eyes and keen appreciation for all that affected her daughter. She knew of her love for Walter, and the whole of the solitary life became concentrated upon that one scheme of the marriage, and the union of Craigburn and Dalmahoy. Never a shade of doubt as to the realisation of the plan occurred to her, until the revelation came that it was not to be. Then the revulsion to disappointment made her hard and relentless. Having had only one thought directing and sustaining her narrow life, she was too old to learn submission, to condone faults and to forgive, when the fact became known to her.

But she was shrewd and practical in most things; her agent and grieve found that, when they came to discuss business with her. There was not a grain of romance in her nature; therefore Walter's marriage to Teenie would have appeared to her a piece of unpardonable folly, even had there been no question about Grace; but when Grace was •involved, his conduct became in her eyes criminal, and meriting the severest punishment. She knew nothing of sentiment, but she was full of devotion to her daughter. For her sake she would do what neither pity nor a desire for her own comfort could tempt her to do.

So, the natural shrewdness and the love for Grace moved her now. She spoke abruptly—

" Get up, and take a chair, wise-like."

Teenie obeyed silently, her heart quite

still, under the impression that she had failed as utterly in this mission as she had done in her attempt to run away.

" That's better," continued the dame, adding sharply, and as if it were a subject of personal offence, " but you're not looking well —what's wrong ? For heaven's sake, don't faint—I hate people who faint. There's no use in it, except with a man, maybe. There's a smelling-bottle yonder on the table : take it ; smell it—get better, and listen to me."

Teenie was obedient, but she did not get better, and she was very weary. Dame Wishart was pleased by this ready compliance with her directions.

" That's better ; you're not such a gowk as I thought you were. Now let us see if we can have a sensible chat. At first I was going to ring the bell and get you taken away ; but you don't seem to have much nonsense about you, and so I'll speak to you."

"Thank you," said Teenie quite indiffer-
ently, for she was now hopeless.

If she had been scheming to propitiate the
eccentric old lady, she could not have done
better. The dame was always suspicious of
any one who made a fraise with her.

"Good; now hearken to me. I don't like
you—do you know what for?"

"Yes—Walter Burnett married me."

"Just that. Well, my brother Dalmahoy
and Walter came to me, both begging for
help, and I refused them. Then you come,
as if there were any chance of your succeed-
ing when they failed. What made you think
of it?"

"God knows; I came without thinking, or
I would have known that the journey was
useless. You never can guess the despair I
felt before I could come to you. The
thought stirred me that you might not be so
very hard, and I came. I'm sorry. I'll go
now."

She got up to leave.

"Sit down," commanded the dame, and she obeyed mechanically. "I said we were to have a chat, and mean it."

The dame was sitting up, erect in her chair, her features fixed in an emotionless gaze, which seemed to exert the power of mesmerism over Teenie. The latter made an effort, and spoke—

"What have you to say?—you refuse my prayer. Very well; we are done, and I can go."

"No, I have not refused, and I want you to tell me what I am to do."

"Me!"

"Yes, you."

"In what way?" she cried with new hope; and then doubtingly: "Ah, madam! don't make me suffer more than you can help; it cannot do you any good, and it may be death to me."

"I am meaning you no harm; but you shall decide between us. I'll tell you everything. Suppose your father had lived for—

there's no saying how many years—in the notion that Wattie was to marry you. Suppose he toils, and plans, and thinks, and arranges, all his life, so that it may serve you and Wattie when you are married. Suppose there has been nothing in the world for him but this marriage—that his very life hangs on it, and that some fine day Wattie comes to him and says, ' I've married somebody else, but I want you to help me '—what would the skipper say ? Would he say, ' I'm sorry for you ; there would have been no need to ask me for help if you had kept your bargain with me ; but I'll help you all the same as if you had not upset the whole plan of my life ?'— would he say that ?"

Teenie felt her heart beat quickly, then stop, and begin again more violently than ever. There was a brief struggle with herself, for she saw clearly what the dame meant, and she would have liked to answer falsely ; but she could not.

" No, he would have been angry—he

would have refused his help," she cried, with
a sensation as if her heart and brain were
bursting with the wild throbs which agitated
them.   But she had spoken truth, and
although it involved her own despair, she
experienced a faint sense of relief.

" Very well," said the dame coldly, "you
have told me what I ought to do."

There was a curious silence in the room—
silence, and yet the breathing of the two
women was distinctly audible.

Teenie bowed her head as if in resignation,
and rose to leave the room.

" You see it's not my fault—you cannot
blame me," cried the dame.

" No, it is not your fault—there is nobody
to blame, but me."

With what a weary hopeless voice she said
that, and how heavy seemed to be the weight
of that blame which she took so bravely on
her own shoulders !

She was at the door—paused, turned back
to Dame Wishart, who sat watching her

curiously. The girl was better than she thought! But when Teenie returned, she hastily seized the smelling-salts as if to be prepared for a scene : hysterics—or a faint, which was equally abhorrent to her.

But Teenie was very quiet.

" I want to shake hands with you, Mistress Wishart, and to say good-bye. We are not likely to meet in this world again, and I wish to part friends. Try not to think very hard about me ; I had doubts, but I could not know that I was to be the cause of all this trouble."

" And what will you think about me ?— that I'm a cruel old witch that has neither heart nor gumption, and that ought to be burnt ? Is not that it ?"

" No, I will try only to remember that you are the mother of Grace."

The dame searched her face suspiciously, as if to detect any trace of deception or cajolery. But she discovered none, and so, briskly she said—

"You have told me what I ought to do; now I'll tell you what I'm going to do—I'll find the siller for Dalmahoy, so you need not be downcast on that score."

"What!"

"I'll find the siller for Dalmahoy. Grace wants it, and so I agree, now that I've had a chat with you. You're not half so bad as I thought you. Don't say a word but go and tell them, and if one of them comes to thank me I'll refuse to do it. It's Grace who wants it done—it's Grace's doing. I would have seen you all far enough before I would have done it. But she's a fool, and I'm half-minded to set you down as another. Come and see me again this day six months. Go."

Teenie stood dazed and dumb; she was like the condemned one who obtains pardon at the foot of the scaffold; she could neither understand nor realize the position at first; and during the whole of the dame's eccentric address—delivered with great volubility—she scarcely moved.

The revulsion of feeling from despair to joy was too sudden, and the first thing she did was to give a big hysterical sob, to seize Dame Wishart's hand and cover it with warm kisses of gratitude.

This the dame resented fiercely.

" I hate hysterics, and the whole cleckan of woman's ways," she cried, and rang her bell violently.

Grace appeared.

" Take this gowk away, or she'll smother me," was the dame's command.

" God bless you !" gasped Teenie.

" You have consented at last !" exclaimed Grace, her pale beautiful face illumined as if by sun-light.　She had never doubted that her mother would consent.

" Away with her, or I'll take back my word."

" Come, Teenie," whispered Grace, and led her out of the room.

" Ods my life !" muttered Dame Wishart, settling herself on the cushions; " they made an awful steer about it ; but I feel the better o't. Maybe I'll get a nap now."

Teenie made a great effort to control her emotion, and only touching the hand of her benefactress with her lips, went out of the room quietly with Grace. But as soon as they were in the parlour—only Pate looking on, wagging his tail and grinning with his ugly mouth as if in entire sympathy with the whole proceedings—she clasped Grace in her arms.

" It is all your doing—you have saved us —God bless you—you were made to be a comforter of those who suffer. You bade me hope—it would have saved me many a pang if I could only have believed in you. I never can thank you enough, Grace, for this, but I shall try to love you more and more."

This gratitude was painful to Grace. She had pleaded with her mother, and implored her to do what she had now done : but she had never been able to obtain the concession, although she was sure that it would be given in time to serve her uncle.

" I am very, very happy, Teenie, that you are relieved," she said tenderly, "but you must not give me more credit than is my due. I did try to get my mother to yield, and she refused ; then you came—she saw how you were suffering—she felt how brave you were, and saw how bonnie you are, and she yielded to you, not to me. She is not hard, Teenie, although she is very stubborn sometimes." •

" I shall never doubt that, Grace. Now I must run and tell Wattie—it will make him blithe. You have saved us again, Grace-- your life must be a glad one."

" It will be so if I see you happy."

They parted : there was no shade of doubt between them now ; sorrow had knit them so closely together. Teenie would have been ready to lay down her life for Grace—admiration and gratitude so filled up the measure of devotion.

# CHAPTER XIV.

## "THE BRAIDER GREW THE SEA."

O it was all settled; there was to be no sale at Dalmahoy, and the Laird would be able to carry out at leisure his multifarious schemes for improving and reclaiming land, and for the discovery of minerals. The latter was his great dream. As yet he had realized only a few specimens of very doubtful ironstone; but he was positive that there were rich seams of coal and iron in the earth, if he had only time and means to pursue the search vigorously. It was beyond question that there were valuable quarries of granite, and with these alone he saw an immense fortune in the

not distant future, if he could get money to
work the quarries, and to introduce his new
system of polishing the granite.

His mind became more deeply immersed
than ever in these speculations, as soon as he
learned that his sister had consented to ad-
vance the money requisite to relieve Dalmahoy.

" She's a sensible woman after all," was his
comment, without apparent surprise or extra-
ordinary elation.

He thanked Teenie as warmly as if he
owed his release to her; and she was un-
speakably happy. After all, her weary flight
from home had not been without its use in
the service she had desired to render; for it
was this flight, as Grace told her, which first
shook the resolution of Dame Wishart.
Teenie knew how Grace must have been
imploring her mother to yield, and she
could easily guess what use she must have
made of the story of her running away, in
order to bring the dame round to the point

of altering her decision not to help the Laird.

They were going to be very happy now; everything seemed to be shaping into a path of quiet and contented life. Mr. Geddies had resigned; Walter would have the full stipend. He had not told her of the objections raised to his appointment, because he could not without explaining matters which for her sake he desired to keep out of sight. She only knew that all was well with them, and promised to be better. Then her father would come home in good time, and he would repay Dame Wishart, and then she would feel so proud as well as happy.

She walked with Walter in the garden, and pointed out to him the various alterations she intended to have made next year. The rose-bushes were to be transplanted to a place close to the house; the "rasps" were to be moved more towards the wall, and the straw-berries were to form a large centre-piece, surrounded by geraniums. She intended to

have such a lot of things done for next summer, that there would be no garden in the
country at all to be compared to theirs.

He could not tell her of the possibility that
they might not be the tenants of the house
next year; he did not dream of the change
there was to be before the winter had
passed.

He saw that she was still very much excited
—feverish, even—and did not wonder at it;
she had endured and suffered so much within
the past few days. He entered into all her
little projects with good will; he shared her
hopes, believed in her plans, and was ready
to help in their realization with all his heart.
But he could not avoid feeling uncomfortable
when he looked into her face, and saw that
its brightness was almost unnatural.

" What a pity!" she cried, standing beneath
a large apple-tree; " the leaves are becoming
brown already; and, see, some are beginning
to fall."

" What then ?—as they fall they suggest to

us the glories of another spring and summer."

" I dare say," she answered thoughtfully; " I never cared about these things in old time, but somehow the brown leaf makes me sad now, and the prospect of spring does not relieve me—there's a gloomy winter between whiles, you know."

" But then we have bright fires and merry stories to make the winter nights short; we have work, and hope to make the time pass too quickly rather than slowly; and we will rise up in the spring with new knowledge gained to make the summer all the more delightful. I like the winter nights and the snow."

" Because you do not doubt the coming of the spring."

" And you ?"

" I cannot say, and I do not want to think. I am just that happy I could greet. But I will not. Come, and I'll show you how I would like the beds of pansies laid out;

Grace is fond of pansies, and I want to give her a surprise."

" You are always thinking about Grace."

" I cannot help it ; and maybe the reason is partly because I find you are always thinking of her when you are sad."

" Yes."

They walked round and through the garden, Teenie full of her new arrangements and improvements.

He observed that at times she leaned heavily on his arm, and again seemed to barely touch him, as if she were making a mighty effort to show how strong she was. He did not like that, and he liked still less the occasional chills which passed over her.

At length he insisted upon her going indoors, and she submitted. She attempted to nurse Baby, and was too weak—she could hardly lift him. So she went to bed laughing at her own weakness.

" I have been too much put about, Wattie," she said, with a hysterical laugh, " but I'll be all right in the morning. Never you fash about me."

But she was not all right in the morning— she was in a burning fever, unconscious of everything and everybody about her.

It was many days before she became conscious again. The poor child's nature had been overstrained; the journey, weary and futile, then the visit to Dame Wishart, had worn the life out of her, and although joyous excitement had sustained her for a few hours, the moment it was withdrawn she fell down, utterly worn out and helpless. Besides, the fever, which, in her weak condition, she had taken from the child of the gipsies Broadfoot, had begun to assert itself.

She lay for days unconscious of everything around her—the passionate devotion of Walter, the faithful nursing of Grace, and the ever-present care of old Ailie. All that love could do was done for her, and many times the eager eyes of the watchers were gladdened with hopeful signs.

But the hope died out as they listened to her piteous cries for help—she was in a great sea, and the waves were threatening to overwhelm her ; but her father's hand could save her, and he would not reach it forth. Then there were visions of the old life at the Norlan' Head, of the pigeons, and the occasional flights in the boat. Next, there were storms and shipwreck, and her father was drowning, and she could save him if she would only reach out her hand ; but something held her back, and she saw him sinking before her eyes—sinking when she might have saved him, and she could not lift an arm. That drove her frantic, and she struggled fiercely to get out of bed, whilst the hearts of those who watched became sick and hopeless.

At length there came a calm. She remained very quiet, and gave no trouble. She opened her eyes, and asked for Hugh. The bairn was brought to her, and she played with his hands—she was very feeble, and it was with difficulty that she could move her arms. But she seemed to be pleased at the sight of Baby, now a big strong fellow, with a will of his own. He made a grand dive at her hair, but as it had been cut short, he only caught the strings of a cap, with which he was quite content, and began to amuse himself.

She laughed, and hugged him—it was such a pleasure to find that there was anything about her which could afford delight to others. They wanted to take Baby away, after he had torn the cap off her head, and had made several attempts to gouge out her eyes. She resisted, but she was very weak and so they carried Hugh off, screeching with regret that he had lost a new toy.

Then Teenie in her awakening senses began to wonder at the strange silence in the place, and at the dim light.

"Why do you not open the windows?" she gasped; "let me see the garden. I want to get all these rose-bushes moved, and that

honeysuckle is too thick about the door.  We
must have it spread more over the face of the
house.  There's such a heap of things I want
to have done this year.  What a vexation to
be lying here quite useless !"

"I'll see that it is all done as you wish,
Teenie," whispered Walter, his voice trembling and husky; "don't disturb yourself
about it."

"Very well."

The sound of his voice soothed her in the
wildest paroxysms, and she remained for a
long while silent and motionless, after he had
given her that assurance of the fulfilment of
her wishes.

By-and-by she reached out her hand as if
seeking something, and Walter's hand grasped
hers ;  that seemed to relieve her, and she
knew at once who was beside her.

"I'm thinking about those rasps, Wattie ;
if we could get them planted up along the
dyke-side, they would look better than beside
the strawberries."

"Yes, just as you would like to have them."

Another pause.   Then she, quickly—

"There's no word of my father yet?"

"None."

"When you get word of him coming, you must deck me up in all my braws, and we'll go down to the port and meet him. He'll be that glad to see us—but not a bit more glad than I'll be to see him.   Dear old father! he's just gone off on this whaling expedition to get siller for me—as if I needed siller when you were beside me, Wattie!   But I thought it would do him good, and so I said nothing.   Have I been long lying here?"

"Yes, several weeks."

"Lucky he didn't come home whilst I was ill—he would have been upset about it. What a pity Mistress Wishart could not have made up her mind at once to help us.   Is your father quite well?"

"Quite well, Teenie, only anxious about you."

" About me ?—have I been so ill then ?"

" You have been very ill—so ill that we were all frightened about you."

She was silent for a little while ; and then, anxiously—

" But I'm better now ?"

" Oh, yes," he cried eagerly, " you are much better now, and we will soon be out together, running about like bairns, and blithe as bees gathering honey, that is pleasure, from all our old haunts."               •

She was silent for a long while again ; and then, with a restless movement, she muttered—

" Queer how that ballad keeps running in my head, and always the same verse."

" What is that ?"

" Do you not mind ?   I sang it not long ago :—

> " ' And hey, Annie : and how, Annie ;
>     And Annie, winna you bide ?'
> And aye the louder he cried ' Annie.'
>     The braider grew the tide."

"It's a sad song, Teenie, and I don't like it."

"But aye the saddest songs are sweetest. Oh, Wattie, I was that wae when I thought there was to be sorrow and parting between us on account of that nasty siller: and now I'm that glad to think of the bonnie days we are to spend together—in the woods, on the moors, and on the sea: my heart is just bursting with joy, and I cannot bide quiet."

"But you must be quiet—the doctor says so, or we shall never have a chance of the bright days you are dreaming about—my dear wife, I am longing for them too."

The terrible threat which he held out acted like a charm upon her, and she became un-naturally still. By-and-by the restless spirit broke out again, and although her eyes were closed, the lips murmured snatches of her favourite song—

"'And hey, Annie'"—a long pause. Then —"'Annie, winna you bide?'" Another pause; and after, she broke out in a low tone

as if she were dreaming—" But aye the louder
he cried 'Annie,' the braider grew the tide."

Walter felt his heart sink within him.
There was something so weird and prophetic
in the words—she had lingered over them so
strangely, even when she had been well, that
in spite of himself—in spite of all his stern
efforts to suppress superstition of every kind,
he trembled, and was afraid.

What was the mysterious cloud which was
creeping up to him and enveloping him ?. All
his strength was powerless against it ; all his
love failed to help him. There was the dark
mystery, ever present to him, and rendered
the more terrible by her gay words of hope.
He saw the terror drawing near : she saw
nothing. The future was all bright and full
of gladness to her ; she was busy with the
arrangement of the pleasures of the coming
season ; she was full of joy in thinking of the
new buds and flowers which would spring up
under her care.

He knew that the buds would spring, the

flowers would bloom, but she would not see them.　He tried to shut his eyes to that pitiless future : it was there all the same. Turn from it as he would, fate was too much for him, and he was compelled to submit. The flowers she planted she would never see in bloom.

# CHAPTER XV.

HOSE who would have blamed Teenie were silent; those who would have condemned her were full of pity; those who would have remained neutral in the threatened war between the minister and his congregation, became warm sympathisers and upholders. Sorrow had reached out its hand, stirring the germs of mercy in all hearts—almost controlling the thoughts of the people, and directing them into channels of kindness. Even Mr. Pettigrew, as he tied up his parcels of tea and sugar, spoke with bated breath and solemn head-shakes of the state of affairs at the Manse.

Those who loved her, men and women, moved with white faces and in silence to and fro, in the darkness of their fears. She was blithe, and saw no danger. The sunshine which entered the room seemed to fill her with brightness and joy. She was busy with such grand schemes of improvement in the house and in the garden, when she should be able to go about again.

It was this joy and bright hope which tried her friends—the shadow of the future lay so black before them. Walter, Grace, Dalmahoy, and Ailie found it difficult not to cry when she expected them to laugh.

Then came the news that the " Christina " had touched at one of the northern ports. A telegram from Skipper Dan—all well, and the expedition one of the most successful that had been known for many years. In a day or so he would be home, if he had anything like fair wind.

There was nothing more needed to complete her happiness except Dan's arrival.

She sang for joy, but her voice was very feeble. She did not observe that, and she lay with a bonnie smile on her face, listening to the wind, and calculating when it was contrary, when it was favourable,¹ and how fast it was driving the " Christina " home.

About this time Dalmahoy went to Edinburgh. He was absent only four days, and immediately after his return he had an interview with his son.

" Do you smell parchment, and the Court of Session ?" he said smiling ; " I cannot get them out of my nostrils. I have been all this time sitting at the feet of the wise men of the law, and I come back not a whit better than when I departed."

" I suppose your journey was on account of the Methven property ?" said Walter carelessly, for he had no interest in money at that time.

" Yes, and it seems to me confoundedly hard that such a fortune should be lying there useless when there are so many honest folk in sore need of it. On my soul, Wattie, it almost tempts me to become a communist, and to cry out for a new division of the world's wealth. But I am not quite a lunatic yet, and so I am saved from that absurdity."

" Do you mean that you were trying to get part of the money ?"

Walter spoke with an unpleasant quiver of the lip. He did not like the idea at all.

" Why not ?—I was his father—that was no advantage to me, it seems. But on one occasion he wrote to me that if ever I should find myself in extremity he would be ready to share his wealth with me, but not otherwise. He was a queer fellow, but not a bad loon either, and helped me once or twice. He had a spite at me because I did not marry his mother, and he had a most ridiculous tenacity of memory for old scores."

" I quite sympathise with him. I would have had much the same feeling as his appears to have been, under the same cir-cumstances."

" Possibly, and I would not have blamed
you—I am not blaming him exactly—but you
would not have been such a fool as to die
without leaving a will. It was a bit of mean
spite, and showed the lowness of his origin.
Look what quarrels he has caused, see how
he has set the whole county by the ears, and
separated me from some of my oldest friends.
Why, if he had spent his life in planning
vengeance, he could not have hit upon a
more successful scheme than that of dying
intestate."

The Laird looked and spoke as if he had
been cruelly and unreasonably wronged.

" I do not like the subject, father ; suppose
we talk of something else."

" As you please, but you might have the
grace to listen to me—I would not have
moved in the matter on my own account, but
there are others."

" I beg your pardon," said Walter awkwardly and remorsefully.

" Say no more, but listen. I was aware

that none of his father's relations, not even the father himself, had any claim upon the estate. But I had a vague idea—thanks to the necessities that have pressed so hard upon me of late—that those letters of his might, in the absence of a will, constitute a kind of claim ; and so, after much hesitation, I determined to submit the whole affair to the lawyers. The result is—nothing. I cannot make any claim on the score of relationship, and the letters are worthless.

" Then who is to get the money—is that known ?"

" Nobody. Habbie Gowk was the nearest to it ; but he fails like the rest for want of some trifling link in the proof of his identity. The number of claimants is endless ; but none of them can prove kinship on the mother's side with sufficient clearness to be accepted as the heirs. So the lawsuits will go on for years ; people will wear their lives and hearts out striving to grasp the fortune, and they will die lamenting their folly. I shall not be one of them ; I shall be wise in time, and give it up, like Habbie. When one is hungry, a crust in the teeth is more satisfactory than the vague prospect of a fine banquet. The writer Currie still expects to get something for his clients ; but the fortune goes to the Crown, and the Crown will keep it—so there's an end of an auld sang."

" Are you much disappointed ?"

" I am, for it seemed to me that if nothing could be got out of the scramble for myself, something might have been secured for Teenie. It would have made everything so comfortable if she had only proved to be the heiress ; and at one time I really thought she would have got the greater part of the fortune, but it was a mistake."

He had not the least conception of how much misery that mistake had brought to her.

" Did you ever tell her that you expected her to be the heiress ?" said Walter thoughtfully.

" Yes." And the Laird felt that there was something like a blush rising on his face as he remembered the circumstances under which he had told her. He wondered if Walter remembered.

The latter turned away from the subject, and they never spoke of it again. But he saw more and more clearly the cause of Teenie's unhappiness; and he blamed himself much for his blindness—he might have saved her so many sad thoughts. In so many ways he was conscious of failure in his duty towards her, that he could never forgive himself. She had been standing alone, with nobody but him to help or guide her ; and he had devoted himself to his work, shutting his eyes to her needs, and neglecting them.

He prayed that opportunity might be given him to amend the past ; but he could only stand by and wait. Always she had the same loving smile for him, and the same eager question — " What news of the 'Christina ?' "

At last he was able to give the news she longed for : the " Christina" was entering the harbour of Kingshaven. That brought new colour to her white cheeks—new life to her body. She lay listening and waiting for the skipper's step on the stairs.

There was the usual bustle at the harbour: sturdy women packing barrels of herrings, and rolling them to one side, where they formed long rows, duly branded after being examined by the inspector of fisheries. The coopers were busy with hammer and adze, making barrels, or closing up those which were already filled. Vessels of various sizes— brigs, sloops, and smacks—were in process of lading and unlading, or lying up, undergoing repairs. In the midst of all this activity, the " Christina " was slowly making her way to safe anchorage.

Dan, browner and shaggier than ever, was giving his orders in his usual steady, firm way. His giant form towering over his men,

he was more like one of the old Norse kings
than ever.   Busy as he was, he looked often
to the quay, seeking some one who was not
there.

He had watched every small boat which
put out from shore, from the moment they
crossed the bar; but she did not come to
greet him.   It was a long time before he felt
convinced that she was not even on the quay;
and then he growled at Ellick Limpitlaw, as
if he had been to blame.

Old acquaintances crowded down to
welcome him; but Teenie did not come;
no one spoke of her, and he began to feel
that she had forgotten him.   He made his
way to Rowanden, and there he noted that
the pleasure which friends expressed at seeing
him was mingled with a sort of pity.

" Is there anything wrong up-bye?" he said
to Tak'-it-easy Davie.

"She's no weel," said Davie, understanding
at once to whom he alluded.

Then Dan strode up the hill, full of fierce

thoughts of dire vengeance if his lass had not been well treated.

He met Walter.

" Have you kept your word ?" he demanded—" have you been guid till her ?"

" I have tried. Come, she is waiting for you."

The sorrow that was in his face and in his voice satisfied the father; and the shaggy giant, who had been so fierce a moment ago, was led like a little child into her room.

She gave a cry of wild joy, and clasped him in her arms, kissing him many times; and he submitted bashfully. She was so shadowed by his broad person that he could scarcely see her; but he knew that she was sadly altered. She looked bonnier than ever, but her beauty frightened him.

# CHAPTER XVI.

## OVER THE THRESHOLD.

HE was so merry that he almost forgot his fears. She laughed and cried almost at the same moment, in the joy of seeing him safe home again; and she begged him to stay near her—to sell the "Christina," and never venture to sea any more. Then she was so proud when he told her of the thousands which he had gained by this single voyage, and that another such voyage would make him a rich man. She was proud because now she felt that Dame Wishart could be paid, and by her father! He did not understand to what she referred; but he told her that all he had was hers, and she was just to do what she liked with it.

She was quite happy now, and the future seemed so bright that she found it difficult to be still ; she would have been up at once, but when she tried to rise she found that all strength had deserted her : she could scarcely even sit up in bed.

She had Baby brought to him, and she laughed at the awkward way he attempted to nurse his grandchild; she told him how she had been wearying and waiting for him ; and how, since he had come, she would never allow him to go away again ; she told him how good Walter had been, how faithful Ailie had been, and how the Laird was the best and kindest friend in the world.

So she prattled on, and Dan's heart became the heavier as her mirth became the brighter. She told him all that she was going to do, and all that he was to do : the future was very beautiful to her now, and they were all to be so very happy.

But he understood. He had brought riches to her, and they were useless. The glad day,

which had been his guiding star through
many perils, was never to be his; all that he
had striven for was snatched from him at the
moment when his hand seemed to be about to
close upon it.

Others saw that his face was dark—that he
was gruff and indifferent to them. They also
saw that he devoted himself to Baby with a
passionate tenderness, which was all the more
pathetic because he tried so hard to hide it
from observers. He would sit beside Ailie
for hours whilst she was nursing the child,
never speaking, but watching the little one,
and trying to anticipate his wants in a rough,
awkward, and shamefaced way. Ailie caught
him more than once—when she had left Baby
asleep in his crib and returned suddenly—
touching the fat puffy cheeks with tender
fingers, and looking at him with longing eyes,
as if this were a treasure bequeathed to him
by Teenie. He always looked so uncomfortable when thus caught, that Ailie pretended
not to see.

Like the others, he waited day by day, and the silence in the house became so customary, that no one appeared to observe it. Yet all were listening for the change which they knew would come soon.

Dan took to Grace almost as much as to Baby, and she was the only one to whom he would speak of his sorrow. She was a second daughter to him : to all others he was gruff and unsympathetic, apparently indifferent to the cloud which enveloped the house. Baby and Grace lightened the darkness to him.

Teenie was playing with Baby one day, and Walter was standing beside her. She looked at her husband with a smile.

" Do you know, Wattie, I feel as if I were going to learn soon what lies beyond the sea and the hills. What a queer notion that is, and how the desire has haunted me ever since I was a wee bairn !"

" Perhaps it is ambition, Teenie, which should be kept down," he said, shaking his head with mock reproof.

" No, I don't think it is that—it is just a notion.  Do you mind once you told me that if we went over the sea and over the land, we would just come round to the place we started from ?"

" Yes."

" Was it true ?"

" I think so."

" Then if I go away I'll come back to you in time ?"

He busied himself arranging some flowers which stood in a vase on the table by the bedside : he could not speak just then.

" Dear Wattie," she murmured after a pause, " we'll learn some day all that is strange to us now.—I do love you."

He stooped and kissed her.

" Let me kiss you again," she said.  "There, now take Baby away—I'm weary ; let me sleep."

She closed her eyes, smiling, as he lifted the child, and she went to sleep.  He stole out of the room.  Grace and Dan were at the door.

" She is sleeping — do not disturb her,"
he said softly, and they all crept downstairs.

It was the long sleep. So quietly she
passed away, that they did not know their
loss until some hours after she had gone. Till
the last moment she had been so cheerful, so
full of confidence in the bright future, that
even those whose love made them most
fearful, were cheated into hope, and the
end came as a shock to them. Death is
gentle to its victims ; it is the survivors who
suffer.

The tongue of slander had been hushed
before ; it was silenced now. Walter turned
to his work, very pale and weary, but resolved
to go on with it to the end. He had no
thought of running away now ; he was resolved to remain there, that her name might
be the more respected, and that he might
teach the lesson which his suffering had
brought to him. He might have sought for-

getfulness in change of scene and change of work ; but he preferred to go on with the task which had been given him to do, amongst the people who knew his sorrow and who sympathized with it.

It seemed a commonplace way of doing : but he accepted life in its commonplace forms. Romantic despair would have rushed from the scene of disaster, and come back refreshed, with wounds healed by change. He took up his work and went on with it, just like one of the fishers or tradespeople who have to work, no matter how much they mourn. There may have been unconscious egotism in this, for he knew that his sorrow gave him power over the people : his sufferings gave him authority which he had not possessed before. They listened to his words with new-born respect, and profited by them so much the more.

Her memory was dear to him, and therefore he wished to remain near her ; he knew

that in doing so he was discharging a high
duty to the living as well as to the dead ; and
the vanity which strives to do what is best for
others, is surely wisdom ; in his case it was
more—it was self-sacrifice, for he felt that in
losing her his life had been marred, and his
first temptation had been to abandon the
Church altogether.   Was he tried more than
others ?   He thought of the morning after the
storm, and he said, "No ; I am like those
people ; I suffer like them—let me do my
work like them, bravely and submissively,
under what conditions the Lord wills to im-
pose."

So he did not falter in his work ; and the
people wondered whether this were a man
who was callous, or who was brave beyond
ordinary men.   They listened to the pathos
of his voice, to the touching simplicity of his
words, and they believed in him—they were
grateful to him ; he taught them to understand so many things which had been

strange before; patience and faith became comprehensible in the light of his
sorrow.

Skipper Dan was silent and grim.  What
he suffered no outsider could guess ; but he
suffered all the more that he concealed his
grief.  He made a will—provided for Ailie,
and settled everything else on his grandson.
Then he got the "Christina" ready for sea
again, and set sail after a last longing look
at the simple grave in the churchyard of
Drumliemount.

"If I happen to die on land," he said to
Walter, as coolly as if he had been arranging
about the disposal of a block of wood, " I
would like to be laid there—beside her.
Will you see it done ?"

" Yes !"

" I'm obliged to you."

He pressed the hand of his son-in-law, and
went away.  Success attended him wherever
he went.  The sea was kind to him, and all

its dangers turned away from him. It became
a byword to be "as safe as if you were on
board with Skipper Dan." He found joy in
life, little as he had expected it when he saw
the earth close upon Teenie's coffin; and
when his time came, he knew that his grandson was a wealthy man.

The Laird was one of the quietest and one
of the keenest mourners for Teenie. She
had become very dear to him. But he said
nothing about it; if you had heard him
uttering the driest platitudes in the ears of
Walter, trying to console him with such saws
as—"We must all endure these calamities"—
"We are all mortal," &c., you would have
thought that he was indifferent, if not callous.
But in the quiet moments you would have
seen how sad his face was, how anxiously he
watched his son, and how eager he was to do
anything that might comfort him. Then at
times, when the wind was blowing high and
the big voice of the waves spoke loudly, he
would saunter through the kirk-yard and

linger near her grave, sweet memories making shadows on his face — for there is always an element of sadness in memory.

# CHAPTER XVII.

THE collapse of all the claims advanced to the Methven fortune produced as much excitement as the first announcement that it was waiting for an heir. The best society of Rowanden and Kingshaven was up in arms of indignation against the iniquitous law which—by a mere quibble, of course, and read by the officers of the Crown—withheld the property from the rightful heirs. But the matter was not to be allowed to rest—it was too important, the stake was too high, and purely on public and philanthropic grounds there were to be appeals, and every engine of the law was to

16—2

be set a-going to get the money for some-body.

These engines of the law, however, being expensive to work, and the issues being more than likely to go against the appellants, although everybody threatened loudly for a few days, nobody proceeded to action.

One peculiarity of the case was that people who had been at daggers drawn whilst in ex-pectation of getting the money, became quite devoted friends as soon as they knew they were not to get it, and were charmingly unanimous in their condemnation of the jugglery by which they had been cheated of their rights. They were not at all clear as to who had cheated them, or as to the person upon whom the blame should be cast; so they took refuge in vague charges against the Crown generally, and against the Queen's and Lord Treasurer's Remembrancer of Ex-chequer in particular. They had no doubt that this latter official would pocket a large slice out of the fortune himself, and consequently it was not his interest to do justice to the deserving, although distant, relatives of the late George Methven.

Another peculiarity of the case was the beautiful frankness with which each of the lately expectant heirs declared that he or she would have been delighted if the friend to whom he was speaking had obtained the fortune, and that the speaker had never expected, never even dreamt of, any personal aggrandizement by means of "that poor fellow's fortune," but had been all along interested, simply on public grounds, in the success of somebody else.

"What a lucky thing for us," observed Aunt Jane to General Forbes, over their after-dinner whist with double dummy, "that *we* never allowed ourselves to think of that wretched fortune which has upset everybody. We would have been so miserable now."

"Certainly, we were lucky not to think of it, since we had no chance of getting it."

"Don't you think—hearts are trumps, dear. Oh, you know; very well—don't you think that it is very surprising that Dalmahoy, with all his experience, should have ever imagined that he could possibly obtain any part of the estate ?"

" He's a fool—that's bad for you, I take your queen—but I believe that he was misled by some fancy about that Thorston girl. A fine creature she was, and she ought to have got the money—trump to your ace."

" What, have you no diamonds ?"

" Not one ;" and then, in a duet—

" What a lucky thing *we* did not speculate upon that fortune !"

It was in this manner that the heartburning and bitterness of the worthy folk found vent. Everybody was full of self-congratulation over the indifference they professed to have felt regarding the million that was heirless, and of profoundest pity for everybody else who had wasted time, thought, and money in attempting to gain possession of the brilliant Will-o'-the-Wisp.

Even Mrs. Dubbieside, who had been one of the most eager to create a claim, was grateful for the humility of spirit which prevented *her* from thinking about the fortune (privately she told the provost that he was a mean-spirited creature to allow the matter to drop without, at least, causing the dismissal of the Remembrancer of Exchequer). But she was utterly unable to understand how the bailie's wife could have been such a fool as to upset her household by her greedy and absurd expectations—not to mention the extravagances into which she had launched on the strength of those expectations.

The provost, douce man, kept a quiet tongue in his head, and allowed his wife to abuse him in private, and to play the contented woman in public, as much as she pleased. Experience had taught him that opposition was the ammunition of domestic discomfort.

On the other hand, the bailie's wife was equally surprised at the pretensions of Mrs. Dubbieside, and wondered if the provost would presume to keep up his carriage and its lamps, now that there was no chance of his getting any share of the Methven fortune.

" But what will be done with the money ?" inquired Mrs. Shaw of her husband, who, being a banker, was supposed to be well informed upon such matters.

" It will remain in the hands of the Crown, I suppose, until somebody appears with a claim strong enough to win it," he answered ; "and in the meanwhile, Currie, and such lawyers as he is, will grow fat upon the fools whom they can tempt to try to get it. There's no denying, though, it's a hard case, and a great pity that somebody does not get it. It would save ever so much trouble and vexation of spirit during the next fifty years."

" Siller is a dreadful thing," commented the banker's wife, philosophically ; " it's a mercy we have nothing to do with it."

That was the almost universal exclamation ; and the wonder is, considering how thankful all the people were to be saved from the root of evil, that they had been so eager to grasp it, and so spiteful against anybody who seemed to have the slightest chance of beating them in the struggle to possess it.

The widow Smyllie was very much disheartened, and honestly owned that she was so. There had seemed to be a prospect of providing for her children, and it had been snatched away from her. Reason and law were nothing to her. She could not understand why the Crown should absorb such a fortune when there were so many poor people, like herself, who stood in so much greater need of it.

" Do you really think there is no chance for us ?" she said to Dalmahoy, distressfully.

" Not the slightest—how should there be ?"

" And will *nobody* get it ?" She felt as if it would have been a satisfaction to think that somebody had got it—somebody whom she could have abused and vented her spite upon.

" There's not the least likelihood of any of the present claimants getting it, at any rate."

" I don't believe you ever tried, or you might have got something for us."

" Now you are ridiculous, my dear. What could I do ?—I could not make you the man's sister !"

She would not have thanked him if he could have done so ; all the same, she was angry with him because he had not, and refused to speak to him for six months afterwards.

This conclusion to the prolonged suspense about the Methven fortune was eminently unsatisfactory to everybody. If it had been allotted to any one of the claimants, there would have been the comfort of being able to abuse the lucky person ; but when only opposed by an indefinite devourer called the Crown—who could neither feel sarcasm nor suffer under scandal—it was impossible to relieve the heart of its pent-up indignation

otherwise than by pretending to have no indignation to vent.

Habbie Gowk grinned at the general disappointment, and wrote some satirical verses
on the subject, which were published in the
" Kingshaven Chronicle," and caused great
irritation amongst the many who applied the
rhymster's whip to their own shoulders. He
would have been perfectly happy in wit-
nessing the chagrin which his verses pro-
voked, if only Beattie had been there to share
his pleasure. The Laird gave him another
donkey, and it was christened Beattie ; but
the poet was never so frolicsome as he had
been in the old days. He rarely wandered
far from Dalmahoy or Craigburn, and by-
and-by he took up his quarters permanently
at Drumliemount.

Life was not all gloom, however ; and,
thanks to Grace and the Laird, a bright ray
of sunshine cheered the poet. By their aid
the great dream of his youth and manhood
was realized—his poems were published in a

"vollum!" Collecting the poems, correcting the proofs, and watching the growth of the loose sheets into a solid book, filled him with unutterable joy and reconciled him to his fate. He was proud of the poems and proud of the binding—the blue and gold which he had so often fancied. The local papers were very kindly to the poet; and, indeed, there was sufficient in the book to win appreciation from every one who could sympathize with earnest utterance, although the form might be somewhat rough.

Habbie Gowk was happy—more, he was grateful to those who had helped him to this glory. At every new word of praise he felt his shoulders broaden and his head rise, so that he would cry with a child's glee,

"Up higher yet, my bonnet!"

The only regret he had was that Beattie could not share his happiness.

Throughout the time of sorrow at the manse Grace was the guiding spirit; everybody turned to her for help and guidance. Quietly she took command of the house, and saw that all the necessary arrangements were made decently and in order. When the sad duties of the occasion had been performed, she went home.

No one had appeared to be conscious of the gentle influence which had kept everything straight, but the moment she left, her presence was sorely missed. Walter was for some days restless and uncomfortable ; the skipper roamed about the house in an unsatisfied way ; and even Ailie felt that the compass of the house had gone wrong, or was lost.

The feeling, however, wore away in time for all hearts except Walter's. He missed her from the house ; he missed her controlling hand in all her surroundings. He said nothing ; he went on with his work resolutely, determined to teach in his life, as in his preaching, that the often apparently unmerited misfortunes of this life are reconcilable by faith with the common idea of the Christian creed, that God watches over the fall of a sparrow even, and is tender and helpful to all who love Him. He wished to show to his people that there are the possibilities of happiness in every life, if we only know how to reach and use them.

And he did not fail in this; the people loved his calm face, which was full of a divine sympathy, and they appreciated his earnest desire to help them in the common struggle of daily life—to keep the heart pure and the feet clean; but they felt it most whenever sorrow lighted on their hearths.

To Grace he was always an affectionate brother; but as time went on, and he noted the clinging devotion of his motherless child to her, he was startled by an idea which he dared not utter, and which filled him with painful questionings.

She was always the same to him—in all things his loving sister and adviser. She did feel momentary chagrin when there came whispers to her ears mating the young widower with this or that eligible damsel in the parish; but she presently laughed at the rumours, and she watched over Baby with a tenderness for which Teenie must have been grateful; and the child took to her as if she had been his mother. She was able to do this frankly, because she was so entirely unconscious that Walter ever could be more to her than a brother.

" Aye, aye," muttered the dame often,• as she watched Grace moving about the room; " and that poor lass has gone, and I'm here yet. Well, I'm getting on in years, there's no doubt of that, and there's no saying when my time may come. But I'm real glad I did not refuse her that time she came asking for help. I would have been sore fashed now, if I had thought she could have carried a black score against me up Yonder. And she was not a bad creature, either; I would have liked her much if she had come to me again. —Grace!"

"Yes, mother."

"Tell your uncle Hugh I want to speak to him."

Dalmahoy came; but his interview, which was private, ended in his again offending his sister. He left the room saying—

"I'll do nothing of the kind. Leave it to themselves; if it comes about, all right; but I won't interfere."

Then there came a time when Dame Wishart was very ill. Dalmahoy and Walter were often with her. Grace could not be spared from her side for a single hour; and so Ailie was obliged to bring little Hugh over to Craigburn to see his adopted mother. The dame frequently desired Grace to bring the bairn into her room, that she might see what he was like, and how he was thriving.

On one occasion when she had sent Grace for Baby, she turned to Walter with all her old sharpness and penetration.

"Wattie, my man, I am coming near my time," she said quietly, "I mean the time when you'll have no more fash with me. When that time comes, Grace will be alone in the world."

There was command, and yet appeal, in her voice and look. Walter was startled, for she suggested what he would have most desired; yet feared to breathe. But when Grace at that moment entered the room with Baby, he put his arm round her waist, and led her to the bedside, looking at the dame as if expecting her to speak.

"Bairns," she said in her brusque way, "do you think you could do something to pleasure me before I go?"

"Oh, mother," cried Grace, "is there anything we would not do to pleasure you?"

"Then get married; the lass Teenie would wish it as much as I do."

Grace shrank back, but Walter held her firmly and Baby interfered with her movements.

"Thank you, aunt," he said, looking at

Grace tenderly; "you have said for me what I never could have said for myself, although I wished to say it."

"Marry her, then, marry her, and I'll die happy," said the dame hastily, and as if she were anxious to get the matter settled off-hand.

"Grace, I have thought of asking you to be my wife, but dared not. It is your mother who helps me to my only chance of happiness in this life—will you marry me?"

She was dazed and confused for a minute; then she placed her hand in his frankly, giving with it her whole heart and soul.

"Yes, Wattie," she said simply.

The two, with clasped hands—she holding Baby as if he were part of the compact—bowed their heads before the dame, who gave them a fervent blessing.

"That's right, that's right; you're sensible at last.—Now read a chapter for me. Read a bit of Solomon's Song, and stop when I lift my hand."

Walter took the Bible, and read the passage she desired, Grace sitting beside him the while, with Baby on her knee. Dame Wishart lifted her hand when he came to the words—

" For, lo, the winter is past; the rain is over and gone; the flowers appear on the earth ; the time of the singing of birds is come."

THE END.

ILLING, PRINTER, GUILDFORD, SURREY.